DYING IN PIECES
Stories About Jean

Nathan Lindsay

For D.J.O.

DYING IN PIECES

The Party

All of the ashes drifted lazily toward the ground beneath the cascade of streetlamps and this buzzed gathering of friends. From above we must've appeared as a sloppy collection of dancers, performing mismatched minuets and waltzes. Within the rhythmic melee, however, there was the comfort of familiar faces and voices that curled away the dreams the day had extinguished.

The past always seems noble, or somehow admirable, in this way. Youth, in retrospect, is disguised by smiles and careless, freefall evenings where anything goes. As the embers distinguish themselves with their orange, sparkling allure, the exaltation of a bright Summer night elevates the arrogance, and conversations blend with literate depth and patronizing parrying. The truth is that the night always meant the precious light of the workday was done and we could finally play.

We were corralled in Colleen's back yard when Ben took the picture of all of us that night. The white picket fencing formed a perfect rectangle that encased our drinks and secrets. It was always a kind of revelry at Colleen's. The merriment was squeezed within this snug space and no one seemed to break protocol to venture beyond the gated area. We simply sailed between chats, spiraling as life rafts adrift without oars searching for smokes, drinks, or just someone to laugh with.

I used to love the way Jean's frame would cast shadows beneath the colorfully hung Christmas lights that defied the absence of the season itself. Her outline was sleek and slender, stirring with as much flight as the physical form that bore its glistening weight. When she spoke, you could hear the mixture of oblique melodies and clear edges, like songs you never saw coming.

"I HAD to leave work early today. The nausea was mind-numbing…" she bellows above the crowd and clamor. She'd been working the same flower stand for nearly two years. The owners only recently figured out that she was fourteen when they hired her, paying her under the table for her time. Her age was finally revealed because a few days prior, on her sixteenth birthday, Ben and I pooled our money and sent her an arrangement of flowers with a balloon that showcased a sparkling "16". The kicker, we thought, was that she was getting a delivery from another, competing flower stand.

There was an alacrity about her that I admired. She was ready to be there for someone even if it meant dragging her down a peg or two. She possessed a nurturing ear for anyone regardless of where they were in life. Beneath the swift zeal of dancing firelight, she was beautiful, and she barely knew I was alive. I remember standing there that evening, as Ben took his photo, wondering how I could snake my way through the crowd to utter a few simple words for her to hear. *You're beautiful, you know that?*

As the breeze broke through the Summer night, so did my planned resolve. Walking adjacent of her centered position I made my way toward the keg corner for another round before deciding to call it a night. There would be other evenings with Jean, moments when we'd laugh about something the sun had said, or marvel at the rolling waves of La Jolla Shores. All the while I spent my time hoping she'd see something in me she could believe in. I've always missed her eyes beneath the blinking lights of Christmas lies.

A Rolling Sonnet

It was our first time and I staggered, heavy
with nervous energy, the soft spread
of her legs, unwound along a lovely levee
capturing the thrill of each breath and thread.
Laying down with her was as nurturing
as opiates, intoxicating the depths within.
Her indiscreet arched, angelic angling
plucked desires with rolling ease. Her leg
braced, then quivered with tangy tease
of tremors formed from lonely long hours.
We felt saturated in a lovely satin sea
as swirling tides seemed paced to devour
tensions from shameless silhouettes spun
and cradled by some perfect curling ocean.

Ford Galaxy

A 1964 Ford Galaxy is basically a boat on wheels. They're difficult to steer and maintaining anything remotely resembling a straight path while driving one is bordering on futility. The experience must be similar to controlling a sixteenth century sea vessel. Regardless, Johnathan thought it was the coolest car he'd ever laid eyes upon. For him it spoke of an entirely different era when jazz was just as hip as rock-n-roll. For Johnathan, a 1964 Ford Galaxy was akin to jazz.

Jean felt differently about jazz. She loathed it all entirely. At sixteen she was enmeshed within the sounds of Circus Lupus, Modest Mouse, Unwound, and Drive Like Jehu. These were the modern incarnations of punk rock for her. While she hated the music that Johnathan was attracted to, she was jazzed about the Ford. It was large, white, and possessed a cool blue interior that immediately captured her senses. In addition, it was large enough to have sex in and that was a huge plus from her vantage point. For Jean, the 1964 Ford Galaxy was basically a hotel room on wheels.

Sexual adventures aside, I know how difficult this car is to manage on the road because I had the opportunity to take the helm one night as the designated sober driver. Johnathan wanted to take Jean out for a night and they both wanted to get drunk on whiskey. I was living with my friend Rob at the time in an apartment near Florida Street and University. It was an awful two-bedroom apartment that we shared with millions of roaches. They were at least nice enough to scatter when we turned the lights on. I typically ate out.

Johnathan called early that evening, "Howard, would you mind driving us around tonight? Jean and I want to drink, but I don't need the piggy hassle."

"Sure. As long as you don't mind me bringing my roommate. I'm not keen on the notion of playing chauffer."

"Yeah, that's fine. Also, would you mind picking up the whiskey? I'll pay you when you get here."

"Shit. Okay, no problem."

I told Rob what we were up against for the evening. Neither of us had much money and I wanted to put my cash in my own gas tank instead of a bottle. There was an Albertson's up the street from where we lived. Their liquor aisle hugged the side of the store that led to the exit. Feeling "cool" we waltzed into the grocery store trying not to seem suspicious, which made us suspicious anyway. We each grabbed a fifth of Jack Daniels and started to trail toward the front of the store. The security guard was occupied with the lines of customers.

I left my car running just outside the entrance. As soon as we neared the exit, we bolted. All I really remember about that moment was a rush of adrenaline and the security guard running outside and yelling "Hey!" as if that would inspire us to stop and turn ourselves over. I sped out of the parking lot nearly hitting someone pushing a cart. Making left turns on University and then Florida Street I quickly got to the Interstate Five North at the bottom of the hill and we were gone.

We made it to Johnathan's in record time. Ten minutes from San Diego to the Clairmont area. Both Johnathan and Jean were in high school. Johnathan's parents were out of town, which meant a little more freedom for him as far as drinking, staying out, and having Jean stay the night. Once there he tossed the keys to his car into my hands. "We're taking my car. It's an automatic, so you should be fine. Did you bring whiskey?"

The three of them opened a bottle and started taking shots and deciding where to go. We obviously couldn't go to a bar, but Johnathan knew of an all ages pool hall in Pacific Beach, so that was our destination with whiskey in tow.

Driving Johnathan's car was no easy feat, at least not as simple as he implied when he tossed me the keys earlier. Even worse, it's annoying to try and get used to the nuances of someone else's car when everyone in the car was getting comfortably drunk. Through the rear view I could see the glowing lights of the city suburbs sparkling across the realm of a mirror. I could also spy Johnathan and Jean making out in the back seat, sensing a pang of longing that I loathed in that second. My peering looks backward quickly found the road in front of us. I felt caught between the seams of something buried.

Johnathan was a great navigator between kisses and expertly directed me to the pool hall in Pacific Beach. Everyone, but me, took a large swig of whiskey before exiting the car and went inside. The aesthetic of the place was bright and there was a mix of dive bar and regulation size tables. Time and balls were purchased at the front counter for the regulation size tables. Johnathan paid for an hour of time and set up our teams. Rob and I would be up against Johnathan and Jean. Johnathan had a fake ID for getting into twenty-one and up shows, so I knew how sorry his game was. I'd never played against Jean, but sorely underestimated her.

"My shot!" she insisted. Her frame seemed to caress the contours of the table as she bent to position herself for the break. Her elbow was high swayed with assurance. With a quick flick of the wrist her cue struck the ball, and, with her first shot, she sunk three balls. Rob and I were flabbergasted. Even sober I could never muster an opening shot like that one.

"I'm up," she joyfully boasted.

We spent an hour and half at the pool hall and the clear winners were Johnathan and Jean. On the way out to the car for more whiskey I sided with Johnathan.

"You knew she could play like that?"

"Yeah."

"Fucking cheat, dude," I smiled.

The three of them finished off both bottles of whiskey there in the parking lot of the pool hall, stalling a moment as a police car casually drove by. They decided it was time for some weed and that was back at Johnathan's house. It was a twenty-minute drive from Pacific Beach back to Johnathan's. Again, I struggled to keep the car steady as I drove this trio of drunks. Johnathan and Jean were making out again in the back seat. Rob was stooped over the dashboard as if ready to serenade the thing.

"You okay there, buddy?"

"...fine, fine..."

I was driving up the hill on Clairemont Drive and made a left turn towards Johnathan's neighborhood. As soon as I rounded the corner the unmistakable red blue sirens flashed their silhouetted beams throughout the car. How did I miss that? Fuck!

I pulled the car over immediately and rolled down my window. The officer got out of his vehicle and turned on his flashlight. As he approached, his light investigated the scene inside. We all looked young. I was twenty-two but could have easily passed for fifteen with my long, blue hair. His first question was directly aimed at Jean.

"Everything all right, young lady?"

"Yep, everything's fine officer," she responded with a gleeful chirp. He inquired as if we had accosted her somehow. I weighed in at 110 pounds on my own and had long, blue hair. Jean could easily take the three of us down on her own. What is this cop's deal?

Then his light focused on me. He asked for my license and, as I handed it over, I explained that I was the designated driver of this bunch and had never driven the car before.

"The reason I pulled you over is because you were swerving pretty bad up the hill."

"This thing's a fucking beast, sir. I drive a Mazda 626. Not the same experience."

That at least got him to smile. As he did, Rob threw up all over the passenger side window. I heard Johnathan say "Fuck!" and Jean giggled uncontrollably. The odor was horrible and hitting me squarely since the only exit was the open window on my left. I looked up at the officer and simply said, "I swear I'm sober."

"Just get everyone home and don't let me catch you out here again tonight."

"Not a problem. Thank you!"

Once back at Johnathan's we got Rob in the house and straight to the shower to clean up. Johnathan was pissed about his car and told me to leave Rob at his house. "He's cleaning up that shit. Not me." Johnathan packed a bowl and we all smoked in the living room while he put on Miles Davis' "Bitches Brew". I loved that album back then. I still do.

Marine Street Piss

This is bound to be a roughly sewn story...

Nestled in La Jolla, California, are an array of wonderful beaches. La Jolla Shores is typically the most crowded and offers choice breaks for anyone with a board. It's an idyllic and often congested area. The water is clear, and waves are beautiful, glistening in the early mornings like an open invitation from Poseidon. As the tides break the white foam seems frothy and exuberant. It's a great tourist destination, as well as being staple for the locals who surf there. However, this tale is not about that beach. This story occurs slightly South of that crowded destination.

At the end of Marine Street is a small stretch of residential seaside possessing some semblance of seclusion from the throngs of that of La Jolla Shores. During the day the crowds are meager. At night it's virtually void of people, save those who live in the area. This was our destination one Saturday night in 1992.

We were gathered at the Go Home. I can't remember who coined the term "Go Home", but it was an apt title for the architecture of the buildings. They were meant for musicians and artists of all types. The rooms within seemed to coalesce and form toward one another, constructing a collection of symbiotic spaces. While one's living space might afford a ten-foot-high ceiling, others were nearly 20 feet and afforded

outlets along the top edges for anyone who felt artistically inclined with power chords. Three Mile Pilot practiced in one
such room for many years.

We — myself, Andy C., Mikey Z, Johnathan, and Jean
— were kicking back in the room next to Three Mile Pilot's
practice space. A large 30-foot-high loft, we could hear them
practice with precision, sometimes stopping mid-song to
make changes or address someone's fuckup. At such young
ages they were serious about their craft and the music that
ebbed through the walls. We were stoned as Pall's melody,
singer of the band, and Zach's bass peaked with one another in some braided form as the words seemed to meld with
the instrument. We constantly retrain ourselves. The space
echoed with Pall's voice fused into the conversation we
were having. We were trying to figure out where to go while
Johnathan packed a bowl in a bong. Taking a hit, he exhaled
"Marine Street."

"What? Why?" asked Jean

"Let's go skinny dipping!"

I'm not sure why this needed any planning of any kind
but, apparently, it was an idea that needed some thought.
Johnathan was kind to me in that moment. "We have to take
Howard though. He dropped a hit earlier. We can't leave him
here to veg out alone."

All in agreement, as the bowl was passed from one to
another, they got ready to go. Jean borrowed a couple towels
from a laundry basket in the adjoining garage and we were
pretty much all set. As they beelined down the hallway to the
exit door I trailed behind, mesmerized by the checkerboard
floor which seemed — to me — to be softly slithering like
small waves of a rippling lake. This trajectory toward the door
led us past their practice space. One down and a hundred to
go, I swear. Each footfall felt never-ending and, somehow, I
was giddy about it and smiling. I loved hallucinogenic nights.
I never had to speak, only watch.

Johnathan's car was parked just outside the Go Home. Jean and Johnathan got in the front seat while I piled in the back with Mikey and Andy. Johnathan made a sharp U-turn and then a right on 9th to find the freeway. We hit a hard dip and he yelled "Dip!" as a mock warning. Once on the interstate toward La Jolla, I marveled at the cars passing by, their lights shrewdly tailing their vehicles. Everyone in the car seemed a kaleidoscope of rainbow and flesh. Speech was impossible for me at that point and I simply smiled and felt the drugs doing their work.

"You okay there, buddy" asked Andy. I nodded, and he let out a hoot of approval.

La Jolla is one of the more affluent areas of San Diego. Nuzzled firmly along the Pacific coast, the homes range from the somewhat modest to the entirely audacious. Marine Street dead ends at one of the more private beaches and, at roughly ten at night, it was virtually free of human beings. Johnathan found a spot to park near the short stairs that led to the beach. The five of us exited the car with a sense of joint comradery that I couldn't quite place. Perhaps it was the acid, but I felt as though I was a member of something singular. We all held the same interests and our humor seemed to mesh together within a sphere of equivocal alignment.

A few couples were making their way back from the ocean's tide as we walked down the stairs. I left my shoes in the car feeling no need for them at the beach and not wanting to get any of the sand stuck on the fabric. It was mid-October and the air was cool, but not so cold that a dip in the ocean wasn't appealing. Near the tide mark they all began to undress. I tried to avert my eyes from Jean but, frying, it was near impossible. Catching me she threw me a smile and squeezed my cheek.

"It's okay, fry boy!"

As her fingers touched me I felt the whole of my body

liquify backward. I'd forgotten I was on drugs. I peered upward for a moment and the orange luminescence of the night sky seemed to be rippled and melting. The water possessed its own aura as each crash appeared to splash ten times over. My friends etched their own forms in the air as time showed itself respectively through each fragmented movement of the contours they carried. I felt both tingling and affluent with my own surroundings. As everyone undressed, I took off my shirt, pulled a pack of cigarettes from my pocket, and lit one. One of my favorite actions while on acid was to wave a lit cigarette forming spiraling designs in mid-air. Andy wasn't getting undressed and I nodded in question.

"I'm just not into this. What's your excuse?"

"I have a small dick…"

This drew a laugh from everyone. I emptied my pockets of my wallet, a pack of gum, and Chinese coin that I carried for luck. I kept my belted pants on because I was just too embarrassed to go full nude in front of my friends. Acid made me self-conscious at times.

Andy stayed behind as we all ran toward the waves. My limbs felt unsure and I couldn't tell if I was actually running, but I was keeping pace with the other three. The waves seemed to caress the skin, and darkness lit all around with an electricity I could barely contain. I was meeting each wave with a dive. I could hear Jean behind me yell, "Howard, don't go too far!" She was always conscious of those around her and the concern for my safety and state of mind wasn't lost. I held firm with the Pacific reaching my neckline and feet upon the ocean floor. A billion lights seemed to pry through my stuttered, wet eyelids.

We were in the water for nearly twenty minutes before deciding that we accomplished our goal. My pants felt heavy with water and the drugs made walking a chore but entertaining as each footfall produced edges of time spliced through physical movement. I needed a cigarette badly. However, on the beach there was no more Andy. In fact, there were no clothes. Our belongings were accosted, and it seemed Andy had ditched us. He even took Johnathan's car. I was pissed because I wanted a smoke pretty bad. The boys were annoyed. Jean was furious being the only the girl of the bunch. I think she felt somewhat vulnerable and that fueled her disgust. Johnathan, not really knowing anything else to do, simply lay down and cursed Andy for stealing our shit. This infuriated Jean even more. Before I knew what was going on, she'd squatted over Johnathan and urinated all over his chest. All of us were teary eyed, laughing, and smiling, at the spectacle of Johnathan freaking out and running back to the ocean to clean off Jean's piss.

Twenty minutes might have passed but it felt like a thousand years in the coolness of the ocean air. As we sat and waited, we were hit by two beams from a car that parked at the dead end of the street. The four of us simply stood there in awe as the light irradiated everyone's nudeness. It was Andy. He shut off the car and exited carrying everyone's clothes and a bag of burritos.

"What? I thought you guys might be hungry. Also, it was fucking boring watching you guys out there. Not you, Howard. How's that little dick?"

"Bolstered", was all I could come up with.

With the introduction of food and return of everyone's belongings everything seemed forgiven. Andy just wanted to pick up burritos for everyone, but didn't want to leave our things unattended. It was a well-meant gesture, but he'd missed the part with Jean pissing on Johnathan.

"Sounds like Jean," was all he offered on the topic.

After we dried and got dressed, we left Marine Street and headed south toward Pacific Beach. Johnathan took a left on Garnett Avenue and started to head inland toward his house.

For me, the world around was still a celestial cascade of color and movement frozen, yet mobile. The trails of people along the avenue were somehow unreal, as if all were made of pastel. As we passed Moose's Bar, Johnathan pulled a bottle rocket from the glove compartment, lit it, and aimed the minor explosive toward the crowd waiting in line. As I watched the people scatter my laughter took over. The kaleidoscope of living young washed over me. As the laughter droned away in the car I looked toward the front seat and saw Jean. The silhouette of her curves lent some comfort in my disseminated mind.

Two-Sided Coin

Her hair was sometimes black. At various points in her life her hair was even blonde or pink, but I preferred the brown that coaxed her hazel eyes. Her best look came naturally and complimented her sense of advocacy, along with that infectious, spontaneous streak. There was once a Deborah Jean Gadzala, or someone like her, whom I love very much.

When I lived on Goldfinch and University I ran out of cheese one day, making the sandwich I was working on seem unappealing.

"I'll be right back!" she bellowed. A half hour later she showed up with slices of cheddar cheese she'd lifted from a Safeway down the street. She loved to steal.

I lost track of her while I was in college, but I never forgot about her. She was my longest running crush. It stung a little bit receiving her wedding invitation in the mail one afternoon. She'd found someone and, maybe, it was time for me to move on with my life. There's no better way to do that than within the confines of college dorms. I drank and did every drug I could get my hands on and, somehow, still left Santa Cruz with a solid 3.2 GPA. I couldn't even tell you half the papers I wrote or what they covered.

She was getting married to a guy named Dylan who played with Crash Worship. Just before heading off to school in Santa Cruz I took a cross country trip with a friend of mine, Charley. We hit all of the 48 states of the mainland within a year. While we were in the South, driving through places like Georgia and Alabama, we'd see Crash Worship flyers posted at local coffee shops. For two weeks we'd missed seeing them by mere days. Jean was traveling with them at the time as one of the dancers of this psychedelic troupe.

I kept tabs on her through college. I'd heard about her pregnancy and Dylan's decision to quit the band and find a profession to support his new family. I actually ran into Jean and Dylan in Hillcrest one evening during one of my Spring breaks. Her son must've been two or three at the time. I remember smiling and feeling a mixture of joy for her life and jealousy that her existence had veered away from mine. She was still as vivacious as ever and her smile melted away all the negatives. She was Jean.

News of her was sparse over the years, but I never forgot her. In 2008 my son was born and, shortly thereafter, I'd heard of her divorce and heroin addiction through mutual friends. I remember being pissed off about her addiction. Newly sober, I sorely remembered how many of our young friends were lost to addiction while she and I were growing up. Using heroin — to me — seemed akin to spitting upon the graves of those we missed the most. Still, I could forgive her addiction because I understood its nature. Through forgiveness, what reminded me of her through forgiveness — who she is and was — was a song by Dinosaur Jr. called "Raisins":

> *I'll be down, I'll be around*
> *I'll be hanging where eventually you'll have to be*
> *I'll just stare and hope you'll care*
> *It's only everything standing in front of me*

> — J. Mascis

It was a song we grew up listening to and the sweet, complex melody of dissonant guitar and fractured vocals always reminded me of her — always. There was a beautiful dissension to those songs that I unconsciously attributed to the askew position I held with her. I loved her then, and she barely noticed me in corners. Now, she was in trouble, but I didn't know how to get a hold of her or where she was living. I would have no idea the scope of her tragic turn until a few years later after my divorce.

One song truly stands out among the others through those early years when I had a profound crush on Jean. The song is "Alone Again Or" by Love. The Damned did a version in 1987 that was inspirational but, the best rendition of the song — in my opinion — was done by Calexico in this century. It's ironic that I got Jean to appreciate Calexico while we were together and, yet, I never played that cover for her, nor did I ever tell her how much it carried me through our youth. Regrets.

I nearly suffocated when we finally did reconnect through social media. From what I saw she was trying work a program, just like me. I'd waited years to share my feelings with her and didn't really want to wait. Falling in love was easy because of our shared history together. There was an underlying mutual respect that hadn't dissolved through all the moments of time. It was as if a placeholder were concocted just for us.

I listened to her journey. The torment of addiction. The rape that naturally comes with prostitution. The control that men can yield over women. She both loathed and loved the life. She'd grown accustomed to it, as a soldier who's seen too much for anything within to be undone. She was still the feminist. She was still the activist. But she was more now. She was a prostitute, an addict, a cutter, a kleptomaniac, hypersexual, and someone who'd been arrested twice for possession at the risk of her own children. She had a co-occurring disorder. Addiction compounded by severe mental illness. One of the most devastating facts I came to know is that there is no ideal treatment for both mental illness and substance abuse. The two are treated definitively separate, yet one does not exist without the other. Insanity fueled and flamed by a candle lit at both ends. Change is needed, or the outcome is surely death.

She always spilled her coffee... always.

Unwound

During the eighties and nineties, it was almost a crime to be involved with the punk rock scene. It seemed as if we were hassled as much as gang members. Shows would often get shut down early and it was hard for bands to book at local venues in San Diego. In response to some legislation that passed within the downtown area, Jean and a few of her friends formed the 917 E. Street Collective. The idea was that by considering themselves an organization, rather than a venue, the cops couldn't shut down shows. Jean made tons of business cards and all you really had to do to be a member was to have one and sign at the bottom. I still have my card.

The collective didn't last very long and barely anyone remembers it except for those who played in that space or knew someone who founded the organization. The space itself was small and probably all their collective could afford. An average living room is larger than what that retail space was. The floors were stained cement and there was a high roof beam that hovered over where the bands typically setup and played.

I attended a few shows there, but the only one I remember clearly is Unwound. I remember the crowd spilled out into streets for this Olympia band. It was more than Jean expected, but it was also exciting for anyone squeezed within that small room to see Unwound in such a confined space.

I remember it was a clear, Spring night and the orange haze of the city skylight crafted tangerine shadows as many of us gathered outside, huddled and smoking. Add to this a mere five-dollar donation at the door and the appeal was enormous.

I barely remember who I was talking to and it probably doesn't matter. I never said much back then anyhow. Jean saw me and knew how much I loved Unwound. She grabbed me by the left hand as the embers trailed off the right hand holding the cigarette. She was leading me through the packed crowd toward the door, so I flicked my smoke at a passing car figuring someone else would take the blame if it stopped.

"I got you covered, hon", she told me.

Her small frame bulldozed its way through impossible crevices of a shoulder to shoulder spectacle. She led me straight toward the front and right in front of the singer. I was elated. They did sound checks for about ten minutes and then opened with "Nervous Energy":

I'm sure of myself
So, don't get distressed
I'm sure of myself
Put me to the test
I sit here waiting, trying to kill my day
It's you I'm shaking for, my nervous energy

— (Unwound, 1993)

Later in life, as we strolled through Balboa Park on our second date, this memory would seep through to our conversation. She wore red heels, black mesh stockings, and a pinkish blouse. Her hair was in a bun, as if something pulled straight out of the 1950's and she wore an iridescent red lipstick. Her skin was a pale white from the foundation she used, and she spent the entire show sitting on the bannister rail above the band basically vigorously rocking out. There were a few times where I thought she might actually fall.

"How do even remember that night?" she asked incredulously on our second date.

"I was peeking up your skirt through the whole show."

Feathers

There's a picture of you within
the archway of our old home.
You stand, poised and peering
through the edge of your sunglasses.

Your pink dress seems to the drape
heavenly down around you,
exposing your knees and a pair
of shoes from that pristine
collection of yours.

Behind you is the soundless
entry way to our bedroom.
Along the left wall are three,
rectangular shaped patches
of brown feathers arranged
from high to low.

I've copied this consoling formation
within this new home you've never visited.
And yet you're always here.

I'm sorry I moved from our old house.
The ghost of you taxed my sanity
in the worst ways. Like slow motion
replay blanketing the baseboards.
I hope you know… always in love.

I was at Bay Recovery. My second attempt to quit abusing the pain pills that my doctor had prescribed for rheumatoid arthritis. I had a serious crush on the boy I was sleeping with, Wayne. He was less enthralled but gave me the best orgasms of my life. Dylan knew something was going on with repeated texts and calls between me and this youngster tipping him off. Bored of my life — and sex — with Dylan I thought I was in love. I just struggled to remember the kid's name.

Tired of my drama, my relationship with the kid was the last straw for Dylan. He informed me that he wanted a divorce on October 8th, 2004. I remember the date because that was the day my life essentially ended. I freaked out, feeling naked without the comfortable protective blanket my marriage to Dylan had provided. Deciding to approach a kid I knew was dealing heroin I entered the bathroom with this creep for what I knew was the first of many shots. I went into heroin addiction with my eyes open. I knew what that first "shottie" meant — an irreversible descent into a hell of my own design. I felt it was what I had earned with my many failures. That was truly the beginning of a multitude of mistakes.

The rehab tested me the next day. Apparently, my pinned eyes alerted them to my graduation to harder drugs. The test was obviously dirty and they kicked me out. Not completely heartless, or maybe conscious of how much money we had paid them, they sent me to the Alvarado Parkway Institute (API) for a detox and psych evaluation.

It wasn't much of a kick. If I felt any withdrawals I don't remember them. But I played it up in order to secure a pre-scription for Sub Oxone for when they discharged me. API's discharge planner took pity on me and got me into Bethesda, a sober living in South Park.

I honestly tried to get things straight, but my roommate was also an opiate addict. Broke, she needed my money and so she took me to a shooting gallery and introduced me to a man I'd see every day for the next four years — my dealer, Javier. I can see that I wasn't as subtle than I would become in later times. The sober living took another dirty test from me. One bad decision and I was once again without a place to stay.

I started to feel desperate, and, feeling the cold wind, that loss of the security blanket that Dylan had become through marriage and seemingly charmed life, I realized I didn't have a place to go. Most sober livings require a clean test before they'd take you, so that was out. I was dirty and ignorant, at a loss as to how I'd take care of myself. Again I turned to a man to protect me.

I'd met Doug at Bay Recovery. He was from a wealthy family in New Jersey. Knowing he had a spare room in his La Jolla condo I called him working hard to mask the fear in my voice. It's not cool to show desperation in the drug culture and I instinctively knew this. I believe it was fate, or maybe it was his greed that made him take me in. I didn't realize how underhanded he truly was until six weeks later when he tried selling me for drugs. He picked me up dressed as a woman. I tried not to show my shock or amusement. He was a very ugly woman.

He'd been up for nine days, keeping his high going by stripping the apartment his parents had furnished from high-end furniture stores and pawning them off. Largely incomprehensible, he told me he'd just spent the last of his money on the eight ball he had in his pocket. Still green I was scared of driving dirty. He swerved all the way to a liquor store on Market. There he instructed me to go in and request two "flowers". Unaware that I was actually buying crack pipes I complied.

Driving wildly, we retired to his condo. The complex was beautiful and well-manicured. Greenery discreetly hid the parking lot, as if camouflage were a part of its inherit design. It didn't prepare me for the state of his home. Stripped absolutely bare, it held only a single queen mattress on the living room floor, a cardboard box and an antique lamp with no shade. It was also kept at a frigid 45 degrees. I was to be thankful for my coat, using it consistently for the next year.

He introduced me to crack that first night.

I loved it.

KennyBoy

Rancho Santa Fe is a small, elite district within the county of San Diego. Professional athletes, corporate CEO's, lawyers, and advertisers all make their homes within this seemingly isolated and idyllic community. On El Camino Del Norte there's a sharp, upscale coffee shop that feels as if it's run by the wife of one of the wealthier residents, donning an odd array of pseudo Native American garments and artwork along the walls. Next door, the realty window boasts current estates up for sale, the cheapest of which is 1.2 million. It's a quiet and secure environment to reside in… unless you've been struck by borderline personality disorder and addiction.

Late one Thursday afternoon, David pulled into the estate he shared with Jean and their two children to find her digging deep holes in their front yard. As he got out of the car, the neighbor ushered him across the street and spoke to David discreetly.

"It's been like this for most to the day, David. When I asked her why she was digging holes she told me she was looking for her face, so I left her alone. Betsy and I have been keeping an eye on the kids though. You've got to do something. This is the third time in two months".

"Thanks, Derrick. I'll figure it out soon".

David knew the mixture of opiates she took for back pain weren't conducive with Effexor and Lamictal. The result was that her manic, borderline personality became so pronounced that nothing about her made sense. He was exhausted and spent from worrying about the kids every day while at work and just couldn't live this way anymore. He had to send to her to a rehab center to ween her away from the opiates. He loved her and this choice wasn't easy. Her allure was like being in love with sin, as if it were a lurid, palpable amalgam of something both wicked and lavish. She was irresistible trouble by design. She was his wife and a mother, and she needed more help than he could give.

After a few phone calls that evening he found the McCallister Institute in La Mesa, just off the 94 Highway. They accepted his insurance and had a bed available the next day. David called work and let them know he wouldn't be in the next day. He then called his mom, who lived nearby, and asked her to watch the kids. After telling her what he planned to do her response was "It's about time!"

Talking to her about the entrance into rehab proved the most heartbreaking of experiences.

"You're giving up on me?!"

"Of course not! I love you. The kids need you. We need you whole and, right now, you're broken. You've no idea the helpless position you've placed me in."

"You?! What about me? So now what? I get dumped off at some rehab and you file for divorce. Fuck you!" The tears broke her resolve in the last moments. She knew he was right, but simply didn't want the help. She was afraid he'd find a happier life without her. She felt distant and alone. There was no peace in her mind and she felt out of place even as he tried to hold and console her. The next day she hugged her children for what seemed like hours and then rode in the passenger seat, balled up and shaking, all the way to La Mesa.

The institute had a seemingly holistic approach to recovery. The problem didn't rest within the drugs or drinking but stemmed from other areas or triggers within the psyche. Their attitude was that the afflicted person needed to change aspects of themselves in order to find peace and serenity from their addictions. An Alano Club nearby was also requirement for the patients and they visited meetings four times a week under supervision.

They frisked her during check in and she cried. She felt lost, violated, and abandoned with David looking onward with stoic resolve. Checking her bags, they allowed her psych meds to remain, but the opiate prescriptions were turned over to David. Sharp objects, such as her razor and tweezers, were also confiscated and remanded to David. "I love you," he said as he kissed her moist cheek. She said nothing. She felt anger and fright. She also felt nothing and, somehow, far away from him.

The first couple of days proved excruciating. She was dizzy and numb as her body felt the shock and withdrawal of zero opiates. On the third day, she called home and spoke with David. She was crushed to hear the ease of tension in his voice and devastated to hear the voices of her children. She'd felt she'd lost them all. The weight of her mental illness mined itself within her soul keeping the conversation quick and superficial as possible.

"How's Mr. Witherstone? I know he thought I was a batshit crazy in the front yard. Tell him I'm sorry."

"I'll tell him." David was unable concentrate on what she was saying. It'd been almost a week and he could hear the progress in her voice, but there was something more nagging him. *What if this happens again? I have to think about the kids first.* Eventually, for the children, he'd have to prove her fears correct.

The next day he met with an attorney. He had her served while she was in rehab two days later. The world around her shattered and the shades were drawn tight. All she wanted to feel was nothing. She knew the kid across the hall was holding, but she had no money, so she made a deal with him. He keeps her high on heroin and she fucks him whenever he wants. After a while she even started to like it a little bit. David hadn't touched her with such verbosity in years, so it kind of felt nice.

A month had gone by and it'd been almost three weeks since she'd been served the divorce paperwork when David came to visit her. "I don't want to do this, but I don't know what else to do. The kids saw everything you were doing, and they were scared."

The reality of her mistakes, especially her most recent one with the kids, drilled to the core, crafting her first scar. The gravity of understanding that, had she stayed clean, there might've been some hope for the her and David, jolted her into a dense sadness. A few days later she'd been caught high because her behavior elevated to something erratic. She was caught attempting to pick through the carpet for a pill she'd dropped. Her Effexor. She was emphatic and insistent in her underwear and wouldn't respond to the night nurses. The next day she was informed she'd be leaving the program.

She called Johnathan, an old boyfriend from high school, to come and pick her up. She had nowhere to go. Her mother had already made it clear that, if she were high or holding, not to bother coming to her house. She had Johnathan drive her to Mission Valley, to a restaurant called Junk House Gastropub. David hadn't yet cut her card off, so she bought them both lunch. As soon as they were done ordering, she could feel that itch slither across her skin. Excusing herself, she made it to the restroom to get in a hit. She must've been a long time, because Johnathan had already finished eating and was getting ready to leave her.

"I'm not supporting this shit, Jean. I'm not into it. You need help." He simply walked away and left her. Deserted and forlorn, she sat at the table dissolved to terrified tears.

"What you doing kid?" came through a rough-rounded voice from behind her. "What do you need?" he asked, noting the pock marks and fresh scars. That was the first time she'd met KennyBoy. He looked around sixty and, the way he was dressed, she made him out to be one of the cooks. She'd later learn that he was part owner of the restaurant along with being one of the counties' largest crack and heroin dealers. He earned enough to be counted among the respectable and was able to keep both lives partitioned enough to stay afloat.

Not knowing how to survive the streets, he taught her what she needed to know and took it out on her in kind. Her life shifted and swayed with double-dark sides from that moment on. She learned how to maintain a distance and resolve from the normal others, while nurturing her addiction and seeing "dates". Kenny would set up "dates" through the restaurant. Sometimes they were simply eager young men but, mostly, they'd leave her battered and broke. The consequence fueled her addiction. David remarried within a year of filing for divorce and her kids barely knew her anymore. I deserve this, she told herself.

You Working?

It was with some trepidation that I got out of the rental car and stepped into the hotel parking lot. I hadn't eaten a real meal in over a week while at McAllister Detox and had been kicking methadone so hard my entire body ached. It was ten in the evening and I welcomed the reprieve offered by the cool Fall breeze. I'd been up for two days and saw myself entering an unknown environment with an unknown element with a relative stranger at my side. The pool dispelled an alien light, filtering through the half dead palms along the wide, trimmed foliage, adding to the general surreal state that recent deprivations seemed to enhance.

The connect had set us up with an opportunity, so thank God for the connect! He took one look at my face — two weeks in to a hard kick — and just broke us off enough to get and stay well for the night. We had no money for dope, food or a room. This opportunity to play "secretary" to a working girl who couldn't get unstuck long enough to work for the speed she slammed hourly seemed an easy way to meet the basics while we figured out our next steps.

Reaching the door of what was to become our temporary home, my partner reached out and tapped the door. A response took so long coming that I thought that we had the wrong room, it was no longer an option, or we'd been tried and found wanting through the keyhole sped through my mind. Finally, a raspy young voice yelled to wait 1 minute that slowly turned into 3 before a mid-young skater/gang thug unlocked and opened the door.

The room was typical for a 1 ½ star hotel. No bedbugs, but no phone and the bedspread was decorated with cigarette holes. The thug that answered the door introduced himself as "protection for the girls". He said his name was Anthony. The working girl was beautiful from the neck up, but crazy... the kind of crazy you can smell, it's so pervasive. Every movement she made was affected and studiedly languid as she informed me of my duties. Basically, I was going to set her up on BackPage, take her calls, pretend to be her and whisper "you know you want me..." to her clients until they showed up. At which point she'd get up long enough to do the date. Basically, all the hard parts.

In the middle of this impromptu listing of my duties I was able to interrupt long enough to exchange names. Everyone in the room seemed so spun out that such cordial nuances were foreign affairs. Up to this point my companion kept his eyes on me, weighing whether he should get the bags from the car or not. He was waiting for a sign that I was going to fall in with this gal's plan or learn enough from her litany to realize it made a hell of a lot more sense for me to take my own show on the road. Reluctantly, I realized, that I could either take her crumbs and be her servant or I could do all the aforementioned tasks and keep the money myself. We were desperate.

My companion, Joseph, began asking a few questions. Logistics mostly but some were pointed enough that she knew that we knew we were getting the raw end of the deal. Her response shocked the shit out of me, without looking at him or addressing him directly, she told him quite clearly that he was present on sufferance and that he was not to speak. So I left.

She chased me into the parking lot and convinced me to stay. She apologized to him and begged me to be her "secretary". I agreed but had my own reluctant plans already in place. I'd learn about the online posting process by securing her a few jobs and then begin working for myself. So, that's how I ended up working again.

Methadone Motherhood

She felt as if she were trapped within humankind's clutch. The world around her seemed to bear down upon, sending her signals that led to a panicked frenzy she could barely provide a name or word for. Lying on her disheveled bed she could hear the twins shrieking at one another on the other side of the door. All she yearned for was peace within, so she wouldn't explode her mind of misery upon them. Then she needed to drive to Fashion Valley for her daily dose of methadone. It's April first. This must be some kind of joke.

Peeling herself from the comfort of her bed she stood up, naked, and stretched. As she pulled over a summer dress the hard wood floor caught her eye. Yellow with peonies, she pulled the dress over her head and allowed it to drop cozily upon her body's bare skin. Still half asleep, she unlocked and opened the door of her room.

"What the fuck!" she bellowed and shook. "Can I wake up just ONE morning without the two of you at each other's throats?"

Ally was the first to speak. "Chase won't let me have the remote. I don't want to watch Ninjago."

Chase broke in with, "It's my turn to watch…"

Before he could utter another breath, Jean grabbed him by his hair and pulled on it, so he'd follow her steps. She realized that, at two years old he'd never had a haircut and was it in an unruly state.

"You can watch your show later. Right now, let Ally have a turn. We're going to the back to see Uncle Apple." She could feel Chase's resistance to all this as she pretty much dragged him out the front door and made for the trailer in the backyard. She didn't care. She wanted the madness between the twins to stop so she could make it to Fashion Valley for her methadone. Chase's unruly with packed curls. The temptation to pull at it hit every time the twins fought. On his best days he looked like a very shocked Einstein. With Chase in tow Jean knocked on Uncle Apple's trailer door.

Apple was the third of four children. Jean was the eldest, then Pat, Apple, and Abby. She could hear rustling from inside the trailer as its occupant attempted to navigate toward the front door. As it opened Uncle Apple leaned out with a smiling "What's up?" She loved her brother more than any one on Earth and that was no exaggeration. Without him she wasn't sure she could stay clear of those triggers in her cognizance that always led her toward a path of heroin, crack, and prostitution, and away from her children and family. *How many times have I broken my own heart?*

"Apple will you PLEASE shave Chase's hair. I know it's early, but I need to get to the clinic, so I can get my dose."

"No problem. Come on little man! This is going to be fun!" Apple was always the jovial sort and the simplicity of his presence offered some contentment from her broken consciousness and addictive yearnings. Once the three of them were back in the main house, Jean began to scramble through the clutter for her mom's car keys. Mom was out of town, so she had carte blanche over her vehicle. At this very second her mind was bombarded by a whitewash of complicated, compressed, and convoluted emotions that ranged from paranoia to utter fear. Her skin itched, and she found it difficult to keep from shaking even though she felt awkwardly numb all over. She was shaking and needed her fix.

After she found the keys she left the house with Ally in front of the TV and Chase in the kitchen with Uncle Apple somehow excited about the prospect of losing his hair. Why don't my children love me enough to feel comfortable? She knew the answer but allowed the thought to migrate somewhere beneath the need for her morning dose at the clinic.

The road to the clinic was a straight five-minute shot down the hill from Linda Vista. She made the right turn on Friar's road and sped toward the entrance of the clinic nearly a half mile down the road. The driveway to the office complex that held the clinic was steep and it overlooked Fashion Valley Plaza. As she parked the car she was surprised to actually take in a spinning breath of the valley below. In that tiny, proportional moment her addiction was non-existent and all that mattered was that haze of sunlight splashing across the vale below.

The clinic was the first floor of the office complex. As she walked into the foyer she was relieved to find only three ahead her. She never spoke to anyone. She simply waited. Today wasn't her day to speak to the doctor and she was eager to get her dose and get home. She noted the one man in the room gazing at her with an odor of Christ! I want to fuck that! She'd left the house without bothering with underwear or a bra. The silhouette in the sunlight produced a once-over for anyone who'd cared to notice.

Once she got to the window she showed her identification as the nurse found her dose along the table behind her. A 100 mg dose that she hoped would taper to a lower milligram someday. But she was fresh out of the treatment center the hold from heroin was still robust. It would be another month before the clinic would award take homes and lowered doses.

She made her way back up the hill and back to her mom's house. The lines of the streets seemed — to her — like breadcrumbs guiding her to her destination. As she sped through crosswalks into the neighborhood she could feel the methadone doing its job. A rush overwhelmed her crafting a certain detachment from the world around as she reminisced about the real thing. This is the danger of methadone. It's a powerful opiate, but just nowhere the substitute for heroin. A thought entered her mind. *I might have to call KennyBoy for some hard white. Crack would ease this tension.*

As she entered the house she found Apple cleaning the kitchen of hair and Chase on the couch with his new dew. It was brilliantly short and she found herself sanctified by the handsomeness of her son. He was adorable. Jean started their breakfast, which consisted of waffles, peanut butter, and syrup. It was nearly eleven. *I am failing them.*

It was hard for her connect to Chase. She'd been the cause of a divorce and lost the right to interact with her two children from that marriage. Chase reminded her of her oldest boy, Johnathan. Today, she would make a concerted effort to find some connection with her children. With the help of Apple, the three of them raked the piling leaves in the back yard. The twins had fun roaming through each immaculate pile, only to be sharply disappointed to learn that they had to reshape what they'd damaged. Overall, their smiles and laughter had a certain contentment that Jean found rare in her life. Her moments slowed that afternoon to a rhythmic pace where her soul danced rather than ached.

As the evening approached and the simple pizza dinners where thawed and served, the effect of the methadone felt warry and wanting. She struggled to capture the high as it softened. Her fingers shook, and she could barely read the book the twins had picked out for the nighttime tuck-in. The methadone seemed absent. After the children were tucked in, and Apple made his way back to the trailer behind the house, she erratically searched for and found her phone within the pile of blankets on her bed. She dialed until the voicemail re-cording echoed in her ear. With a desperate, wabbly voice she said, "KennyBoy, it's Jean. Listen I need eight tacos right away and don't worry, I got what you need. C.O.D. Call me back soon, okay?" "Tacos" was code for grams. The hard white of crack was all she could envision as she lay in wait for Kenny-Boy's return call.

Jean's Confession: Target

I'm down to 21 milligrams of methadone and I don't think it's holding me the way it should. I crave heroin, or even crack, to quell the later parts of the day when the methadone begins to wear thin. One of the things I was worried about earlier today was how I was going to buy clothes for the twins. I thought about shoplifting. The high is something I miss. It's exhilarating. I did bleach my hair yesterday. Against the blue black it was before there's an orange tint to it that I like. I have to laugh at myself. I have nothing else.

I hate detoxing off methadone. I started detoxing after I left the McAlister Institute and it's been week after week of fractured moments. I feel like I'm stuck in a sort of mental traction as the doses go lower. My brain and body want heroin so badly that I can barely focus on the twins, which is why they're in dire need of clothing. Thank goodness for my brother, Apple.

Earlier today I went to my scheduled counseling appointing at the clinic. Jennifer — my counselor — came outside while I was smoking and spoke with me for a few moments. I was forced, through some wings of honesty, to let her know that not only had Joseph relapsed, but that he was in jail again. I also told that I believed that relationship was over. If he cared about me he wouldn't have landed himself back in jail. She couldn't contain her glee. The prospect that this threat to my sobriety was out of my life for now was exciting for her.

Anyway, my brother. I didn't get my money the way I'd expected and ended up paying my phone bill with the last of my money. It was then that I started freaking out. How could I forget the twin's needs? What sort of mother am I? I've barely been a part of their lives since the day they were born. I've spent these years using and whoring instead of being the mother they need.

When Apple called earlier I was frantic and exhausted from crying over my mistake. He told me to just head over to Target and he'd meet me there. Once there I told him about my plans to shoplift, so he kind of took over from there. We got what the twins needed and then he did something truly wonderful. He had me choose a pink fleece jacket for myself. The entire bill was $170.00! I love my brother! Chase got a Lightning McQueen jacket and Ally got two pairs of leggings and two long sleeve shirts for school. One of the shirts had a monkey riding a giraffe. The jacket is perfect for light or heavy weather. It's well-made and expensive. The entire affair was tantalizingly out of my budget.

I'm disappointed that Joseph fucked up again and went back to jail, but I'm grateful for my brother. All I wanted was my boyfriend to be happy and heroin-free, but that's not going to be the case. As much as I want him, I need to remember what I need first. I need to keep tapering off the methadone and stay away from Burt and KennyBoy. I hate the thought of detoxing while incarcerated. I didn't cut myself today.

Broken Finger

As she cleaned Jean's room in the basement a hundred thoughts, melted and coiled, within Grace that she found it difficult to focus on the task of cleaning her daughter's life from the room. Each liquor bottle, every pipe, and the stack of used condoms under the bed simply infuriated her. Jean had been taking clients and using with her own children in the room next door. She hated the addiction, but she loved her family even more. It took all her resolve to kick Jean out of the house the day before.

Jean had been good for almost two years. After the twins were born she was ordered to Kiva — an in-house drug treatment program. Graduating from that she moved back in with her mom, began attending school, and even got a job at a local flower stand on Genesee Avenue to help with bills. Yet, the last six months that stability began to wear down. She quit her job and started skipping classes. She knew she was getting high but had no idea she was "working" out of the home until she cleaned her mess that day, finding the piles of used condoms under the bed. How could she do this with her kids only a few feet away in the next room?

"You think I don't know what's going on downstairs? Look at yourself! You can barely form a sentence and I can SMELL alcohol all over you!"

"You want me out?! Fine! But I'm taking Ally and Chase with me!"

"Not a chance, missy! They deserve the best parenting and you can't provide that in any way, shape, or form, where you've been heading!"

"Fuck you!! So now your taking my kids?!"

Jean hastily packed two medium duffle bags with clothes, make-up, the heroin she'd gotten from KennyBoy, and outfits for clients. She stormed up the stairs without a word to the twins or her mom and slammed through the front door. Her intent was to catch the bus to Oceanside and find Joseph, her boyfriend.

She dragged her bags two blocks to nearest bus stop and waited with tears in her eyes. She was frightened and hated not knowing what was going to happen next. She was ashamed at being caught by her mother, but she knew no other way to make enough money for the twins. She was trembling beneath an August sky.

She caught the bus that would guide her to Mission Valley where she could transfer twice to catch the Coaster to North County. The last time she spoke to Joseph he was staying at a weekly on Highway 101. Once in Oceanside it took her almost two hours to find the hotel. By this time the sun was setting to the West over the beach city and she was itching for a hit.

Once she found the door to his room he answered her knock with a nervous "What are you doing here?" Jean could see the remnants of some other girl's panties and dress on the floor.

"My mom kicked me out", she said sobbing.

"Okay, let me get rid of my friend. Hang on."

She waited for about ten minutes and it was obvious that the girl who emerged didn't set high prices. She had pock marks on her face and arms, a sign of smoking too much crack. She must've been in her thirties, but it was hard to tell with the obvious, overt signs of addiction.

Once inside Joseph held her and asked if she came empty handed. Of course not. They cooked the heroin over a spoon and filled two darts to a halfway mark. Joseph's arms were still in decent shape and barely bruised, so he opted to inject the dragon into his left arm after Jean had tied him off at the bicep. Jean was less fortunate. Her veins where weaker and couldn't handle the prick of a needle. She injected her half in her left thigh. It took a little longer to kick in, but the effect was the same. They both sat quietly as the heroin did its work. After twenty minutes Joseph said "You'll need to work tomorrow. We need the money to keep this place, I want to pick up some hard white. Bring them back here though. It's safer and I want watch someone else fucking you."

"Okay, babe," was all she could muster. She both hated and loved having to work. She loved it when Joseph watched and her addiction to sex was as pronounced as her addiction to anything else. At least with Joseph watching she could avoid worst case scenarios, such as being stabbed or robbed. They partied into the night, drinking cheap gin and taking hits from the crack that Joseph had left. They partied and fucked until the early morning hours.

At ten in the morning Joseph tried to wake her up with a hard slap on the face. When that didn't work he broke the pinky finger on the left hand. The pain and jolt of that break got her up quickly and tearful. "You need to get out there get us some money if we're going stay here! Get dressed!" His demeanor had changed from the understanding and fun of the night before to one of business and what needed to be done.

Jean got dressed and set her limping finger herself, wrapping it with scotch tape from her bag. The staggering spasm of the break was almost too excruciating, so she took a shot of heroin to get through the pain. She dressed herself in white heels, a short white mini-skirt, and a pink tank top that complimented her blue-black hair color. She was ready.

She didn't a say a word to Joseph before she left. She was still pissed off about her finger. Besides, she needed to set focus to picking up clients on the boulevard. The best place for this a downtrodden section of the street about four blocks north of the hotel. Once there it took mere minutes for a classically kept up Camaro to pull up with the passenger asking "You workin'?"

"You bet, honey. And I can host. My hotel is down the street."

Once in the back seat of the car, the driver asked, "So how much for two?"

"We can talk business at the hotel." Knowing what she'd learned on the streets she was aware of the possibility of these guys being cops. Cops always try to bait transactions in the car, however, these weren't cops. It didn't take long for her to figure they were US Marines on a two-day pass from Camp Pendleton. They talked to one another in acronyms and with a demeanor of someone who'd been emotionally broken down and built back up to conform to Marine standards.

Once back at the hotel she explained her boyfriend, Joseph, would be watching. That didn't seem to faze them since they were looking to double team her anyway. There wasn't much direction in her life at this moment, only the dread of what comes next. They talked prices for two and what was okay and not okay. Anal was out of the question, but they could double team her for a modest price of three hundred.

Joseph sat in a corner chair, masturbating at watching his girlfriend being taken by two guys. They had a little speed on them, and they were considerate enough to share with Jean, putting her in the mood for business. While on all fours the misery of her broken finger spasmed and she expelled a brief scream over the pain. An hour went by before they were done with her. One of the tricks, Jerry, turned out to be a medic. Noticing her finger, he offered to try and properly set it for her.

"Looks like you tried to set it already. It's not going heal quite right, but this splint and bandage should hold it a little better than scotch tape." It was the first time Jerry had paid for sex, so he was empathetic to Jean's pain. He felt it all somehow a special occasion and gave her his dog tag as a reminding gift.

After they left, she and Joseph fucked for hours. At the boundary of their finish she took a break in the bathroom. A tear shed, but her resolve wouldn't allow a scene. *How did I end up here again? Christ, I miss the twins!* It was the first time she'd acknowledged to herself just how much she loved the twins.

Scars Over
the Years

Her life felt like a series of serrated edges. Each scar that adorned her visage held tales of abuse she'd accepted as her own doing. One scar, near the right edge of her lip told a tale of being tragically naïve and needing a lesson in being wise to the blade, that strip along Texas Street where women could make easy money for car fun. Texas Street, at University Avenue, was the perfect locale for women looking to make a quick buck. The corners featured a twenty-four-hour gas station and a Denny's. The illumination from the businesses was enough to showcase what was being offered by each woman, yet there was enough shadow and brush to make quick hide in case the police cruisers showed up. Texas Street was also popular because it was one of the few connecting roads to Mission Valley, an area of hotels and shopping malls just down the hill from Texas street. This meant that many of the "dates" were only in town for a brief stay and might even host. On this particular evening Jean's goal was to earn a quick eighty bucks to cover the next hit and her hotel room near eighth.

It didn't take long for someone to pick her up and he seemed like some giddy college kid who was simply caught in the novelty of picking up a girl on the blade. There was something off about him and she looked for the first thing she always noted — a door handle or a way out. Neither were there and, after she'd gone over prices, his laugh became nervous and frantic. From behind her another set of college arms held and bound her. They drove her to Shelter Island and, at knife point, took turns, clocking her jaw, and fucking her until there was nothing left for her to give.

They were brutal, entitled kids who felt this was owed to them. Women were the lowest common denominator, Christ, she thought, just don't let it hurt too bad this time.

They left her there, near the Sheraton, where she could call her pimp and connect, KennyBoy. About an hour later he showed up with a pinch of the dragon to take off the edge, along with clean darts. He had an idea of what happened through her slurred, swollen speech. The next morning, she woke up to him on top of her, pistol whipping her across the face then forcing the muzzle through her teeth.

"You need to get over that old life and harden up for this one. Get it?

"Yes," she murmured through the pistol protrusion. The scars kept coming, but she forgot the taste of that muzzle.

French Toast & the Customer

The smell of Don Baldwin from the night before drifted and lingered, surrounding her like some foul, contaminated aura. As the trolley pulled up to the Fashion Valley station, Jean checked her large, tan rose bag for the money from Baldwin that morning. The dope-sickness and the lack of sleep were gripping her skin and it stung with fierce yearning. She counted numbers in her head, and a tranquility caused by those hundreds lead to moderate composure, and then to a mindful memory of Baldwin's stench the day before. She had left with him the previous afternoon for a date and had fallen asleep after he'd passed out in the room at Civic Plaza in Mission Valley. She knew the rules well enough to wait until he was passed out before taking the money off the nightstand and placing the wad of cash in her bag. The reek of his seaweed nut, still drifting along the ridge of her mouth, forced her into a chaotic sleep just so she could evade the memory of her time with him.

Just before heading to North County to see her kids for her supervised visit the sight of the clock pierced her already caustic senses. I'm fucking late! She wasn't exactly surprised after being up for three days on crack. When she awoke, however, it was to the mouth-watering aroma of room service French toast and coffee. What luxury! Dazed from the first good rest in days she groggily checked her phone and found 17 messages from Burt, her connect and sometimes pimp, each message grew progressively irate.

Apparently, Burt had called the connect to come over at the exact time when she was supposed to return to National City. Primarily composed of a Hispanic population, National City was somewhere between a ghetto and lower middle-class dwellings, and surrounded by the districts of Chula Vista to the south and Barrio Logan to the north.

Burt's apartment didn't cost much, but it was her derived income that kept up the residence. Not only was he a pimp who worked for Kenny Boy, but he as a notorious gambler and crack addict. She'd forgotten to tell him about her scheduled supervised visit with her two oldest children that day. When she wasn't around, and he had no money, the connect threatened to cut him off and only deal with her. Knowing he hadn't a penny, she was resignedly frustrated and sullen to realize that, yet again, *my money is not my own.* Not a penny for her kids and, once again, behind on her child support.

Leisurely she finished the golden triangles of breaded ambrosia and then began to stress. Her hands shook, body trembled, and the tears made it impossible to finish this fine breakfast. Burt was going to be so pissed at her and might even put her out again, keeping all her clothes to sell to the other girls for hits. She didn't know what to do and she was exhausted from life.

Rule number 76 of being a whore, she thought, cracked within the stage of that moment, *never cry in front of tricks. They are paying for a good time, not drama.* But Don wasn't a bad guy. He just smelled atrociously rotten and vowed to help her. He gave her 900 bucks extra and dropped her off at the station that would take her directly to North County this morning. She was already an hour late.

The archaic sports theme adorning the stained walls seemed oppressive, aged, and blemished, as if it somehow paired itself with the chestnut haze dangling over Oceanside, California. She entered the room looking around earnestly for her two oldest children, Johnathan and Esther.

She hadn't seen either of them since the divorce from Dylan became final over three years prior. Since then, failed stays in drug rehabs — like Kiva — and the birth of her new twins, life had been a series of irrational sweeps. The birth of the twins resulted in her return to Kiva after her blood work revealed the heroin she was using just before their delivery. Through her addictions, and the bends her choices created, wholly organizing her life was impossible and paying for court ordered supervised visits, such as this one, was usually hopeless when hotels and drugs took precedence. This was the first visit she could afford. Maintaining a firm grasp of reality through a smog of mental illnesses was blotched by the beguiling shackles of a life she both despised yet needed to survive. At least this is what her brain had attested and proven to her.

The sports antiquity of decaying posters lining the walls felt like some bitter reminder of recent dates and escorts she'd grown accustomed to over the past year or so. Photocopied reflections of men wearing jerseys and sweatpants saturated the moment with disgust over rapes and begging for anal.

While the walls didn't seem to wreak with foulness, the space seemed to penetrate her senses. They aligned themselves within her dope-sick mind, applying that August stench of recent men. Their sweat, grunts, and demanding undulations nagged at her unnervingly. Their appetites shook her with turmoil even during the loneliest of moments in their absence. Her fingers trembled as she shut the door behind her, tremoring as she loosened her grasp of the gold, metal knob.

The supervising facilitator sat in a sullied, cobalt (or was it black) easy chair, with coils and frays seeming to come alive as the bottom draped the thinning, apple green carpeting. This young, modern woman sat in the far corner of the iridescently lit room, not seeming to notice Jean's arrival within the small sea of other families mulling about the plainness of the small space. Office spaces for visitations always held some tacky motif to make visitations more comfortable.

This coordinator was thin, with pink highlights that matched the full, bright pink of Jean's own bowl cut hair. Jean pegged her to be twenty-four... twenty-six — maybe. *A fucking intern logging hours toward a credential or degree.* Jean hated her already but allowed her eyes to wander and search the room for her children, or even David. As she scanned this den Jean noted the intern's notepad, busy beneath the small, silver pen, recording each oversight and instance that would later affect the lives of the children and parents wandering the room, engaged in bland, banal activities afforded by the drabness of this managed cave.

Jean's thoughts began to flutter backward, to Don Baldwin. Though he was a nice enough professional gentleman in his late fifties, his afflicted and unfortunate malodor remained sealed to her clothes and skin, as if a disgraceful collaboration had formed between the idea of filth and vicious realities that formed her daily life. She could feel the putrid flavor of him braiding through her thoughts as she fought to focus on finding her children's faces. His foul, semen fueled halitosis had somehow found its way into her precious pudenda, slithering along her skin to annex an odor to her clothing that she wished, at this moment, didn't exist. Looking downward, beneath the hem of her skirt, she also craved a change in footwear. She still donned the topo suede, over-the-knee, high-heel boots she wore for many of her customers. She also remembered she hadn't showered that morning.

Through the heroin-haze of this dawn mist she spotted Johnathan, her oldest, crouched before a plum bookcase against the far wall. Just above him hung a poster of Steve Garvey, the white creased paper marking a path along his Dodger uniform and smile.

We're in San Diego! They can't afford to at least put up a poster of him wearing a Padre's uniform?

"Johnathan?" Her voice vibrating with apprehension. She wasn't sure her son would recognize his own mother, with her pink hair, thrift store denim skirt, and lamentable boots.

"Mom!?" He turned and raised himself just enough to find an embrace as slight, joyed tears fueled his eyes. The salted taste of Baldwin that was still lodged in her throat dissolved slightly as she soaked in her son's elation at seeing her for the first time in two years.

"What are you looking for here?" Her voice still shook, but the comfort of that second seemed to counter the strain of finding a question to ask. After so long, she simply wasn't sure where to begin. Her mind raced and coiled with options and answers. How do I repair this? What have I done? What kinds of books does he like? Does he even like to read? He must. He's a reader, just like me! What was the last book? Oh yeah! Dr. Seuss!

He's eleven now. Don't bring it up. He hates me.

For an instant, her borderline personality disorder and dope-fueled mind synced with fetid self-reflections as her fingers shook and eyes twitched around the room. These men! They're loathsome and wondering how much and how can they get a hold me later. Maybe I can make some money. It's all I am anyway!

"I'm not looking for anything, really. Well I was looking at this one. City of Bones. Ever heard of it? My friends have been talking about it and I want to read it so badly, but my mom," he paused. "Carol." His faced reddened and then he collected himself within that second between the tick of the clock on the wall. "She says it's too advanced for me. Something about murder and weird tattoos."

"She's a bitch, Johnathan. You should get it. Can you take books from here?"

"I don't know."

Before Johnathan could say another word Jean's thin, quivering, yet sure, fingers were stuffing the worn pages of the book between stockings, clumps of jewelry, a goth wig, and dark tethered lingerie within her large, mahogany bag.

"Is that a large rose on the bag? I love roses!" Johnathan remembered their yard in Rancho Penasquitos. Within a sprinkling stage of time a portrait of Jean planting roses near his bedroom window filled his eyes just enough to allow meaning to breathe between them. A mere flash of sturdy connection between mother and son that consecrated and stretched seconds into something uniquely infinite.

"Roses are my favorites! Your grandmother loved tuberoses."

"Grandma Ana?"

"No… your other…"

Before she could correct his understanding of genealogy, she felt the firm, grim presence of David behind her. Esther was nowhere around. Jean didn't have to ask and, at the site of her tremoring frame, her ex-husband explained frankly. "She didn't want to come. I wasn't going to force her."

She wasn't surprised, but the heartache was there. She could sense the facilitator's pen working madly behind in that horrid easy chair. (Mother is clearly dope-sick and supervised visits should continue with reduced occasion and diminished time allowed considering the inconsistent visitations that have already occurred).

She didn't know this young lady, but she abhorred her instinctively. As the three of them made their way toward the door, with her fingers behind her, just above the line of her denim mini-skirt, Jean offered the facilitator a definitive finger. Fuck you!

The memories flooded forward in her mind as they walked outside. The rehab that David had dropped her off at in East County; the divorce paperwork arriving within the week; her first hit after fucking that youngster who had the black she made a bee line for. In that twinkling moment, all accountability for her actions became authentic and tormenting beneath the August sunlight that pierced her eyes once outside the dingy, stucco office complex.

There were no "goodbyes". Johnathan's tears were stalled in the presence of his father but, as they clasped one another with wide arms, Jean expertly slipped the copy of City of Bones in his small, delicate hand and gently whispered: "Hide this. I love you so much." She never wanted to let go, but she knew what she'd done to him already. It was time to go.

She turned in silence, and found the road leading toward the bus stop that would take her to the Coaster Connection back to South County, and then to National City and Burt. The visit was barely fifteen minutes long.

She boarded the Coaster that would turn a quick 40-mile trip into a protracted series of scheduled rail stops. She found a seat as far away from any of the prying eyes of men as she possibly could so that she could soak in and saturate the brief visit with Johnathan. She felt her heart cut, a blister of disfigured memories fuming within a flash of gloom and grief.

Johnathan had treated her like a stranger, as if some new neighbor he'd only barely met, discreet within the vicinity of his father. *God knows I still love David! Why am I such a fuck-up!* The tears sang through her mind like a forceful, booming bell, coalescing with the syncopation of hunger for a renovated history.

As the line moved quickly South toward Del Mar, and then La Jolla, past the point where Linda Vista stood to the East, she contemplated her reluctance to love her twins — Ally and Chase. She noted her fears and her knowledge of herself and the life she CHOSE. She could feel the restless hesitance to offer the twins the love they deserved for fear of losing custody of them someday. She needed to spare them the pain of losing their mother, just as Johnathan and Esther had. She knew that if she loved the twins any more than she did — and lost them — she would find no reason to continue living. The tense authenticity of how her emotions had formed through divorce and lifestyle bit through her with a strangling emanation.

The train approached the stop where she'd transfer, returning to National City to deal with Burt, the twins father. She lumbered for a moment in her suede, heeled boots, as the brakes of the car she stood in halted with screeching assertion. She waited an hour for the trolley to National City. The putrid scent of Don Baldwin from the night before was still hovering around her. She loved this because she knew Burt hated the smell of Don and wouldn't want to fuck her for at least a couple of days. As the trolley pulled up to the 24th Street station, she checked her huge, rose bag for the money from Baldwin that morning. Still there. At least Burt wouldn't punch her square in the jaw for that and, maybe, he'd be in a good enough mood to hook up some hard white to stave off the dragon. The dope-sickness was draining her and she was out of darts and methadone. Her thoughts were beginning to amble and the crowds of men that sashayed past her on the station's platform triggered a concussion along the crust of her skin as her eyes hunted for somewhere to run.

Surrounded by men and the stink of Baldwin still fastened to her skin, she began counting — a tactic her therapist had suggested — to find calmness and peace in the elongated intervals that passed until the trolley's arrival. Once in National City, after the long trip from seeing Johnathan, Burt opened the door of the apartment to Jean audaciously fluttering $700.00 bucks in his face.

"What you got, kid?!" his elderly, Trinidad accent exacerbated and disgusted her every time. One of the many reasons she left his name off the twin's birth certificate.

"I need an eight ball now! Get to work!" With Jean's demand, the other girl living there shot a weary look with comatose, bloodshot eyes. Jean hated living with Burt. She hated that deal of having to fuck him and give him half her earnings from dates, but she had no other options open to her right now. *The tincture that is my fucking life!*

She was tired and drained from the visit with Johnathan, seeing David, the absence of Esther, and Don's stink. The dope-sickness was settling in with a traumatic crash. Thanking God that she wouldn't have to fuck Burt, she made the bed in the middle of the studio by throwing the other girl's discarded clothes on the floor, so she could sit down. This girl (what was her fucking name?!) feigned shyness and went into the closet to dress, or so she thought.

That bitch! She'd come out wearing a brand-new dress Jean hadn't even gotten to wear yet, a birthday gift from Kenny — Jean's pimp, and basically Burt's boss. When Jean protested and screamed at Burt, he simply allowed her to shriek. Or maybe age had caught up to him. Jean eventually pried off the dress from the powdered skin of this delirious and drugged girl, half ruining it in the process. She eventually ran off this worked over girl, watching easily as she cried. Probably because she didn't get to smoke, Jean thought. The mini cat fight had aroused the bastard and Jean's heart sank.

But the epiphany of Don materialized through her dope-sick mind. Burt hated any reminder of what she did to get the money through Baldwin and was getting the dope he expected anyway. She still stank of Don. Even though the smell wretched her own stomach, she refused to shower all day long. Burt kept his distance from the whiff of that nomadic odor for two days. It was a passive aggressive move that she adored and elongated.

One Morning...

She sighs beneath the summer sunlight combating her anxiety under the oppressive dessert heat. The coolness from inside the small, two-bedroom home offers a subtle chilliness as she sits on the porch trembling with her cigarette in hand feeling fortunate for sitting so close to the open front door. She'd moved to Barstow with her kids to be with Howard and his son only two days before. Her memory of the last forty-eight hours felt hazy and dreamlike. When she left her mother's, she'd taken a week's worth of crack and heroin just to make sure Howard wouldn't find anything. She didn't want to be holding when she got to where they were headed. At least the methadone was still doing its job.

As she sat, slightly rocking back and forth attempting to control her thoughts and impulses, she could hear footsteps on the carpet inside. Howard had just awakened. He wouldn't come outside until he'd poured his coffee and found his pack of cigarettes. As he stepped through the threshold of the front door he was immediately attentive to her. She loved the intimacy of the instant, yet she still felt far away from the faith and belief one should have in love. She loved him. She just couldn't understand what he saw in an old whore like her.

He kissed her forehead dexterously and whispered, "It's going to be okay". He held her as his cigarette burned away along lines drawn by the wind. She felt important to him. She felt embarrassed and concealing her addictions worried her. She didn't want to lose him. The urge to use again was plaguing her body. She felt its tug like a mass so dense that it engulfed her heart. So, she shivered with her right knee pumping up and down and counted numbers in her head as her therapist had taught her.

"I cleaned up the coffee you spilled", he said.

"It's not coffee unless it spills", she said defiantly.

All he could do was laugh a little bit at her response. She realizes, in that splinter of a second, that it's one of the things he loves about her. Somehow this pulls her mind back to what's in front her and she tweaks his chin just enough for him close in for the depth of a delicate kiss. Why couldn't we have discovered one another all those years ago? How did I miss him!

Nothing mattered in that brief moment. The influence of emotions heaved and breathed a life into each without pause or cause. They were in love and that was all that mattered.

Cream Pie Finish

She was a sex addict, though she'd never openly admit to the condition. She was already plagued by bipolar depression and borderline personality disorder, along with pronounced addiction to heroin, crack, and meth. Another diagnosis against her would make her feel so much less about herself than she already did. When Howard took a job in San Diego for four days a week he'd left her alone in Barstow. They were struggling financially and hoping to move back home to San Diego by Summer. She knew the work was needed, but she hated being left alone. In addition, it was difficult for Howard to keep sending money to her, so she could make the forty-minute drive Victorville each day for her methadone treatment. She needed to come up with her own plan.

Lying awake in the empty bedroom, beneath the high roofbeams of their cozy two-bedroom home she stared blankly at the ceiling. Remnants of an old lifestyle peaked her realm of solutions, but she needed a front of something in order to work up the drive to dive back into that trade. After a few minutes of contemplation, she walked next door to Chico's house. He'd have what she needed or would at least know who to call.

She knocked on Chico's door. Thankfully he answered and not his wife. "What's up girl?" His shorts hung low to his knees, revealing the grey, faux silk boxers beneath. His wife beater shirt allowed the old English lettering of a tattoo to illuminate his allegiance to 32nd Street. Jean thought the whole attire was silly and juvenile. There wasn't even a 32nd Street in Barstow. His black hair was slicked back with some kind of fake pomade. Jean had known harder people than this. Her old pimp would laugh his ass off at this guy and then beat him for fun.

"I was just wondering if you could get a hold of tina for me."

"No problem. I got what you need right here. Twenty bucks for a taste though."

"Is there any way you could front me until tomorrow? I'm going to be working tonight."

Chico really didn't know what she meant by that, but he knew exactly where to find her. He had no problem kicking down a favor for a neighbor. Leaving Jean at the front door he disappeared down his hallway and into his bedroom. When he came back he had a small bag of soft white. The bag was cute, she thought, with its array of skulls for warning perhaps.

"Thanks, Chico. I'll be around tomorrow for sure."

She couldn't wait for a taste of *tina* before the evening fell. As soon she got through the door she could feel herself shaking and her mind wandered to places that were dark and frightened even her. The guilt of cheating on Howard — even for money — etched a mark upon her psyche. She took two Effexor, a Klonopin, and a Lamictal, to calm herself down. Lying on the couch in the living room she waited for the intensity of emotions to subside. Somewhere, deep in her closet, she still had a pipe from last year. Maybe trying a hit of the meth she got from Chico would put her in a more motivating mood. There were steps she had to take to pull this off and a hit of tina would put her in a frame of mind she hadn't been in for over a year. Or maybe it hasn't been that long.

In the bedroom she reached high and far within the

walk-in closet. Deep in the corner were a pair of folded socks she never wore. Tucked within those socks was her old pipe. She went to the kitchen and pulled the bag from her pocket. Most of it was soft white, but there were rocks to burn. Shaking, she pin-pointed a small rock and placed it within the darker, burned end of the pipe. She lit her lighter beneath this area and sucked in the smoke. She almost came from the sensation. Howard can never know. I don't want to lose him, but I'm desperate.

The computer that Howard had bought for her was in the kitchen and sat on the dining table. As she sat down in front of the screen she peered across the table and thought the piles of paper was building up into something that resembled a natural disaster.

The first thing she needed to do was start a new email account. Using Gmail, she went with the username Sammywillplease. Samantha was her alter ego when she was selling herself and she seemed to have no trouble returning to the persona. Next, she needed to open a Craigslist account with this new email. There must be tons of desperate douchebags in the desert. She figured eighty bucks for an hour was more than fair, and probably all she could squeeze from anyone in this area. With her account set, she posted her first ad:

I'm Samantha and I'm a bored housewife looking for a 6one fuck buddy9. want6 me to Suck 4your Cock? Bbbj? I'm discreet6. No Drama, Drugs or Diseases. 7ohoh Roses? Fetish 5friendly. Everything and anything goes. Lets fuck. Can host.

It amazed her that she still remembered how to post with a phone number embedded within the message. That hammer of guilt, though, was nagging her. She loved Howard.

Gazing at the clock on the wall next to the dining table

she saw that it was nearing 1:30. She had to go and pick up Howard's son from school. Howard wouldn't be home until the next day, so she'd been volunteering to pick up his seven-year-old son on Wednesdays. She quickly found her purse, and the keys to the Volkswagen Jetta, and sped out of the driveway heading across town to where the school was. She ignored the speed limit signs in town, powering a steady sixty miles per hour so she could make it the school on time.

As she crossed the first street bridge she received two text messages from that ad she had just posted. One was from a Dakota and simply said "Hello! Are you available? Can you send a pic? My names Dakota" She searched her phone for an old photo of her in lingerie and sent him the picture. It was one she'd used last year when she needed money to get to her appointments in Santee. Once she stopped at the school she sent a quick message back to Dakota. "Not available right now, hun, but I'll be ready later this evening. 11pm work for you?"

"That should work just fine, babe. What's your addy so I know where to go?"

"I'll send my address later on, closer to eleven"

"How many roses are you after?"

"It's 80 for an hour. Well worth it though."

"I hope you like it rough and dirty."

"Sounds great. I'll send my address around 10pm."

She got out of her car to face the Spring desert heat and began walking to where all the other parents were waiting for their children. Howard's son spotted her before she even reached the gate and came running.

"Dill Pickle," she said, "how was school?" Dill Pickle was her nickname for him, and he loved it, but only from her. Dylan immediately took her hand and said, "I'm hungry."

"I'll fix you something when we get home, okay?"

He hugged her. He felt safe with her and absolutely adored

her. Jean was great with kids, regardless of where her mind-set was laden. She loved him as much her own children. She checked her phone again and saw a few more messages.

Once home she noted the other text message. "Hey there sweetie! I'm in San Bernardino right now but can be in Barstow later tonight. Are you available?"

She texted back. She loved texting. It allowed for a level of short hand and pictures that were more difficult to master through e-mail. "I'm free around midnight if that works. What's your name?"

"Ron. Can you send a pic?"

She found an even more risqué portrait of herself on her phone. She was posing with high heel boots, leopard print lingerie, and bent over for the camera.

"Nice! Can't wait to hit that puss, babe!"

"Great. I'll send the address later on, k?"

"Sounds good, babe. Cream pie okay?"

"Pretty much anything goes."

Dylan was out of the car while she texted back and forth with this guy. He'd already gone inside, dropped his backpack on the floor, and started getting his shoes off. Jean put her phone on silent mode and followed him in.

"How about a peanut butter and jelly sandwich, baby?"

"Oh yes!" was the emphatic answer.

"After you're done eating, we can go over your homework and then you can play games on your iPad for a little while before bath and bedtime, okay?"

"Okay."

The evening was quiet, and she enjoyed working with Dylan on his homework. Howard would sometimes get frustrated with him because he was a little slow to grasp some of the concepts, but Jean held on to patience she'd learned through battling borderline personality disorder. She'd count to high numbers in her head or count a beat on her knee.

Whatever her method, Dylan certainly enjoyed working with her more than his dad. Maybe dad's just don't have the patience moms do.

At bath time she let him pick out his pajamas and get undressed. He gave her a long hug and said, "I love you."

"I love you too, Dilly. Now in the bathtub you go, okay? I've got to straighten up the house a little bit." She considered hiding the pictures of their kids, so the customers wouldn't see them, but then thought who really cares. She went through her closet and found some boots and lingerie that would undeniably earn a hard-on. There was that nagging guilt again and she began to count in her head.

In the past, when drugs and prostitution saturated her life, there was never anyone she was in love with. There was never that one person who involved her heart. Not even the pimp — the father of her twins — ever meant that much. In fact, she loathed him, the beatings, and despised the fact that he was her children's father. Right now, they were in San Diego, enjoying a comfortable environment at her mom's house.

Dylan was out of the bath within a half hour and had already begun to dry himself and put on his pajamas. It was nearing nine o-clock. Time for bed. She gave him a chewy melatonin tablet and found a book to read. It was a book of classic fairytales and she read him the story of Cinderella. He was simply as lost in Jean's voice as father often was. After nearly twenty minutes he was out.

It was nearing ten o-clock, so she texted Dakota first.

"Are you ready to come over hun?"

After a few minutes he replied. "Fuck yes!" She sent him the address and let him know she wouldn't be ready until eleven on the nose. A million, pin-pricked voices were alarming inside her mind. She pushed them out and became Samantha. She became Samantha because she needed to and she felt broken. She felt broke.

At eleven a red, Ford pickup truck with buckets stacked in the bed pulled into her driveway. She awaited on the porch wearing a long coat. Beneath the coat were heels, a silken lingerie outfit that had a ribbon around the back that hung between her crack in the middle. "Dakota?"

"Yep. And you're Samantha. God, you're even more gorgeous in person"

She didn't blush but thanked him for the compliment. As they entered the house, she explained up front that her stepson was sleeping, and they needed to be kind of quiet.

"Understood," he whispered. "I just can't wait to get down on that pussy."

She led him to the bedroom and locked the door behind her. He pulled out eighty bucks and placed it on the nightstand. This isn't his first time.

With Dylan asleep in the next room, she got to work. She took off her coat and let it drop to the floor. His eyes widened at her outfit and she could tell this was going be a quick one. She reached for his belt, unzipped his pants, and fell to her knees, all the while looking up at him to let him know she was savoring every second. For a brief moment she thought of Howard and how this might devastate him, but quickly put the concept out of her mind so she could focus on being Samantha. She needed the money. After a few minutes she pushed him toward the bed. As he fell backward she climbed on top of him and rode.

"Let me take control. I want to make you my slut," he said. He turned her over on her back with ease and railed inside of her. Just before he was finished, he pulled out and climbed above her face and started fucking until he finally came. The whole affair took only a half hour, but she felt he got his money's worth.

"I hate to rush you off, but there's a little one next door."

"No, I get it. Can I keep your number?"

"Sure. If I'm free I'll let you know," she said. He leaned in for a moment. "No kissing," she told him emphatically.

Ron was different. He showed up a little after midnight in a beat up looking Toyota. He had to be around sixty, but it didn't matter to her. Not to Samantha. Not to someone who needed the money. She'd made sure she smoked the rest of the meth before Ron showed up, so she was already in the mood. She could tell this was his first time, so she made a little small talk, told him the rules, and took his money. She went down on him slowly at first, but he was so excited that he pushed her hard into him. After swallowing him he let out a huff that was so loud she thought it might wake Dylan. Thankfully, the melatonin ensured that he was out for the night.

After Ron left she retreated back to her room and scraped what she could from her pipe. She just wanted the taste out of her mouth. She was done being Samantha and just wanted to lay awake being Jean again. After the first small hit she heard a car pull into the driveway. Quickly, she took off the lingerie, put on some sweats, and climbed into bed. Howard had come home a day early. She pretended to be asleep when he walked quietly into their room and sat carefully on the bed. "Hey," he whispered, "you up?"

"Kind of. Why are you home now? I thought you wouldn't be back until tomorrow night?"

"I took tomorrow off. I missed you and I just needed to tell you that I'm sorry for being gone so much."

Tears lightly dripped from her eyes as he wiped them away. "Why is the front door open?"

"I was smoking earlier. I must've forgot."

"I got you something. Remember that antique shop next to Le Stat's Coffee House? I found this for you." He reached into his backpack and pulled out a silver music box ornamented with intricate peacock feathers. It was small and would fit nicely with the collection of small, ornate boxes she collected. "I know how much you love peacock feathers. I couldn't resist."

Slowly, she eyed him lovingly and purely said, "I love you, Howard."

They made love that night, but the spirituality she'd always enjoyed with him somehow felt faded or rusted. Samantha had taken her toll on her and, as she slept with Howard, her mind wandered to the two johns who'd just been in this very same bed. The guilt was overwhelming and unexpected. Samantha or not, she needed to bury this feeling. The next day she paid Chico for the meth, bought more, and asked if he get a hold of any black. "I can get anything you need, girlie." No matter how much she did she couldn't shake the guilt. The thought of Howard finding out frightened her into a drug-fueled dilemma she thought she'd left behind. She'd never been in love as a prostitute. Now she knew what that was like.

Everlasting

There's no everlasting love
when life is never lasting.
I miss you, Jean.
I miss you in that way
that the embers of dreams
try to rekindle themselves
when you wake up from something
so precious and everlasting.
When I wake up, you're not here
and my heart feels void of time.
I miss you, Jean.
I miss you in that way that
dust settles and portraits of
landscapes seem to possess
dreams and futures that have
nowhere to run and escape.
I miss you, Jean.
I miss you and I love you
in that way that faith has a way
of carrying a dance forever and on.

She's Gone

I

This is all memory whether truth or fiction. Memory is often unreliable in its vantage points and details. We attribute ideas and details that were never there to begin with. We imagine the emotional complexity to fill in the gaps between solid items, such as furniture, street signs, or buildings. The Friendship Hotel is memory in contrast. A hotel for those who can't afford much else it stands surrounded by the market of the middle-class. Located on Eighth Avenue in San Diego's Hillcrest district, it's surrounded by eclectic antique shops and a Whole Foods market. It doesn't seem as seedy it as its truth.

The door of the residential hotel opens, and her sultry frame quickly breezes through the entryway as I put my cigarette out and walk up the stairs, welcomed with a firm kiss and those hazel eyes that captured me over twenty-five years ago. She's damp, fresh from a shower, as the sunset catches the sheen of her blue-black hair and her voice cracks quickly and gaily with Did you get your homework done? Who cares? Hurry up! I want you! She pauses as we walk down the narrow, carpeted hallway toward the stairs up to her second-floor room. As I place my hand gently along that curve of her hip I can feel the contour of skin beneath the veiled, olive shirt. I love you, she says as her head turns slightly my way. Room fifteen was just up the stairs at the end of corridor.

The smell of pot drifts through the hall of the hotel. As we climb the stairs it reminds me of my college days at UC Santa Cruz so many years before. The aroma floats through the second floor and beyond each door the stories are far removed from the lives of college freshman. These lives wear donated hand-me-downs and the wrinkles of years added from harsh, unforgiving days where the only reprieve burns away through a cheap homemade pipe.

Her room is small and possesses the pleasantness of a walk-in closet. The tanned stains that drip down the walls barely reveal the Navajo white beneath. With the money I'd given her weeks before she was able to afford a single with its own shower next to the twin bed against the window. Other tenants, with softer incomes, were forced to share the community shower downstairs and the wanting eyes of her neighbors was a disgust she wanted to avoid.

The door closed, I feel her press against me for a longer, deeper kiss and I can feel my day melt away along the lines of her lips. We hold each other in that brief second as the history of San Diego ticks away outside. She holds me there in that moment, next to the bed where she would take her last breaths a little over a day later on a desperate Sunday morning. She cements me there in memory, inside that little room where just two weeks' prior her homeless friend — E. Wynn — raped her on her forty-first birthday after taking a series of pictures she'd use for personal ads on Craigslist. She holds me right there every single night.

II

Deborah Jean Gadzala (Jean or Jeanie to those who knew her) was born June 29, 1975, in Phoenix, Arizona. Soon after her mother's relationship to her father ended they relocated to San Diego where she and I would eventually meet while she was dating a mutual friend of ours. It was the early nineties and Nirvana had broken barriers to the underground music scene we surrounded ourselves with back then. Bands like Unwound, the Melvins, Rocket From the Crypt, and Modest Mouse, found wider audiences in the United States and abroad. The first time I saw Unwound play Jean was the one who'd booked their show. She and a few friends rented a small, empty retail space downtown on E Street to hold shows where kids who were too young for the bar scene could come and see bands play.

On most nights the crowds were local, and the number of people barely ebbed outside the door. When Unwound came down from Olympia, Washington, the crowd was overwhelming, spilling out to the streets and congesting traffic. I remember her hand pulling me through the crowd, so I could glue myself right in front of the singer when they played. She disappeared with her boyfriend after I was settled but, many years later, on our first date, she tested me. Where was I sitting at that show?

"Easy. There was this low ceiling beam just over the area where the bands played. You were sitting just above the drummer, wearing a short, black mini-skirt that had ruffles, or something like that."

"How do you remember I was in a skirt?" she asked with an air of flattered shock.

"I was peeking up that skirt."

She was maybe fifteen at that time, but I wouldn't know how young she was for another year when we shared a house as roommates on Eagle Street. She'd been kicked out of her mom's and was working at a floral stand near Washington Street to pay rent. One evening she came home sobbing and shaking. I could hear her breath heaving from the kitchen and, when we met in the living room, she told me she'd found out her boyfriend — that mutual friend — had been cheating on her with a few of our other friends. Devastated she talked me into buying a jug of gin and I sat with her that night, each of us drunk, emotional, and tearful. I remember the moonlight peering through her window, cradling us with soft shadows as I passed out in her lap. I never told her I had a crush on her back then. I wouldn't get to tell her for another two decades.

III

As the nineties rolled on we drifted apart with our lives, keeping in touch lightly the way friends often do. I went off to college, traveled the country, dated, married, got sober, and had my son. I'd heard she'd gotten married and had two kids of her own, but then news of her simply went dark. In 2014 she emerged on Facebook and I quickly added her, curious as to what had been happening through all that time.

From my end of the screen she didn't appear too adept or interested in the age of social media. From snippets of her infrequent posts, however, I gleaned she'd recently completed a woman's detox program in San Diego and was nervously trying to raise her young twins, children she'd had after her divorce (I'd later learn that her dealer/pimp was the father). She seemed an amateur parent and, lacking confidence and expertise, would post her fears and frustrations about school or meals or tantrums. After reading one of the posts I called her. I remember her voice shaking on the other end as I calmed her through the tail end of a stressful day of losing car keys and coping with hungry kids. I told her about my recent divorce and she talked about her twins. Her older children were living with their father in Carlsbad and she hadn't seen them in almost six years. She was open and forward about the reasons surrounding that lack of contact, explaining how she'd been struggling with addiction to heroin and crack through the years.

I was an adjunct librarian at a college in Victorville during the 2014-15 school year. For Spring Break, I drove down to San Diego and we met at a park near her mother's in Linda Vista. She wore an olive-green cap, red t-shirt, and faded jeans. I spotted her right way across the grassy field and, at our embrace, she commented with a smile I know I plumped up, didn't I? Her eyes caught mine as the action of the park faded. We sat, and she explained that the methadone was where the weight gain came from, but that she was earnestly trying to shed those pesky pounds. I was nervous around her. I felt twenty-two again.

We fell in love within a few weeks. The foundation of growing up together made an easy connection and the inspired, resourceful soul I knew was still at the core of who she was. And I fell in love with her survival. She was candid about her divorce ten years before: the heroin addiction that started in rehab after her infidelity with a young dealer; the life on the streets as a prostitute and escort; the name "Samantha" and who she was for other men; and the crack addiction that was married to that life. The stretch of men who'd held her hostage and robbed her of any value would, as the time between us grew, cause heartbreak and tears for me as she recalled each story.

Her dealer, and sometimes pimp, Kenny Boy, was one of the first men she was forced to trust after a stay in rehab and around her divorce in 2005. He'd be a constant fixture of her life thereafter and a consistent worry for us from the instant we moved in together. Of all the people she knew, his number was planted firmly in her mind and she never forgot those digits. His psychological control equated to a relationship she couldn't easily pull away from. During the early years he'd sometimes wake her up in the mornings with a pistol shoved cleanly down her throat because he felt she wasn't tough enough for the "life". She was conditioned and that "life" held her hostage, never truly letting her go free. She was formed to the chaos, robbed of any ability to believe she was good enough for anything more. The nurturing, loving person she was morphed and curled with a lust to mentally escape reality any way she could no matter the consequence.

Later on, there was J. Kruk., a boyfriend she'd lived with in Oceanside. They spent almost two years hopping from street to hotel as she earned the money they thrived on. Most of the week he'd wake up, crazed from the craving for more crack or black [tar heroin], beat her until she woke, and send her out to earn enough for the room or drugs. Sometimes he'd have her bring the "dates" back to the room so he could get high and watch. One morning she didn't wake up quick enough when he hit her, so he broke her pinky finger to shock her out of sleep. She had to set the bone herself while she was out picking up the next "date" a few hours later. Nine months after hearing this story I placed an engagement ring on the finger next to that one as she softly said "Yes" with full, hazel eyes.

Many of the scars on her face held tales of "dates" gone bad, ending in rape or being thrown from a moving car at three in the morning. She was staying at a residential treatment center in East county after her last arrest. That's where she met her attorney R. Burns. They became "friends" when he offered representation in exchange for "services". After the treatment center she had nowhere to stay, so she lived with him, sleeping on the bare floor of his spare room. She'd have to hide in the closet whenever he had a genuine client or girlfriend over.

One evening she went out for a walk. She wasn't even working, she told me. She'd been up for fourteen hours and, knowing the best way to come down off speed was in University Heights, she took a cab there from Ocean Beach at three in the morning hoping her connect was back from the casino. There was no answer on her phone, or when she scratched on her window, so she decided to grow eighty bucks on the blade (a prostitute term for strolling the most lucrative areas). The second car had barely passed her on Texas Street when she was picked up by an innocuous Honda. She figured it'd be another quickie college student just so turned on that he was picking a girl on the "Blvd." and that'd he'd last maybe three minutes.

As soon she got in the car she had a bad feeling. Whenever she got a bad feeling, and semi-panicked, she checked the first thing she always checked: that the door handles weren't tampered with, so she couldn't get out. The guy was really antsy and giggly in a creepy, nervous way. She became positive it was a bad idea when two arms grabbed her from the back seat. A second little creep had scrunched behind the seat in order to reach around, grab her arms and immobilize her. Fuck, I sighed to myself, at least let it not hurt too badly.

Some dates ended with attempted strangulation and robbery. Others ended on the pavement along Rosecrans after being thrown from the cars of satisfied customers. The array of abuse by "dates" was a constant companion to the life she led to fuel her addiction or quell her inner demons. Each scar revealed the story of her working life or some love she'd held onto with hopes for something more serene or normal. Ten years of trying to get it right through rehab or sober living homes. Ten years of struggling and giving up on the world around her. One time she was committed after being found unconscious on the Green line trolley. She'd taken fifty trazadone between stops because her life was robbed of anything meaningful.

IV

Along with a buffet of drug addictions she suffered from bipolar depression and borderline personality disorder. She took Wellbutrin, Neurontin, and Effexor, as well Klonopin and Vistaril for stress. Co-occurring disorder. There would never be an adequate or routine medication regimen that would hold her steady. At some point the fear and reality inside of her would always be at odds with the reality surrounding her, leading to the compulsion to escape any way she could. She was an addict whose disease was profoundly felt and warped through abuse and self-mutilation.

In February of 2015 I was beginning the process of filing for full custody of my seven-year-old. Jean had pushed for this after witnessing his mother's attempts of having him declared disabled to collect a social security check on top of the welfare and child support she already received. To prep I wanted to familiarize myself with autism, cerebral palsy, and EEG recordings in young children so that I knew exactly what it was his mother was attempting to label him and how best to frame my own rebuttal.

I scoured and studied stacks of academic journal articles, websites, and group forums for nearly a week. Our coffee table was littered with statistics and essays regarding topics surrounding the issues I felt I should know. One day, after carping over something minor, her voice began bubbling over with tears. You can spend hours studying hundreds of fucking journals about your son, but you can't read one article about me! I never responded to her accusation and I would never have the chance to tell her that I had. And I can still feel the mixture of gratitude and sorrow as she suggested we keep our engagement quiet until the hearing over my son.

At the end of the previous summer, just before she moved to Barstow with her twins to live with me and my son, I spent a week studying borderline personality disorder, bipolar depression, heroin addiction, crack addiction, and the effects of methadone. I learned about the process of tapering off methadone, the ways that crack can fuel sex and alter judgement, and the physical signs of both crack and heroin use. I reviewed websites that listed drug terminology and slang. Photographs of pock marks on the skins of drug users invaded my thoughts throughout the week, somehow reminding me of her through concern. I even combed San Bernardino for rehabs and treatment programs that would support methadone patients who wanted off the prescription. I also learned about the withdrawals that align each drug. I was expert inside a week and I learned one thing very quickly: I knew absolutely nothing.

A study on borderline personality disorder conducted by Ulrike Feske, PhD, et al. reveals:

> In addition, the co-occurrence of BPD [borderline personality disorder] and SUD [substance use disorder] is associated with heightened risk for a variety of severe adverse outcomes, including participation in the sex trade; a large number of sexual partners, more frequent and serious drug overdoses, needle sharing; an increased risk for suicide attempts; poorer response to treatment; and more severe psychiatric, family, and legal problems. Thus, BPD in conjunction with SUD is potentially life-threatening. (131)

I wasn't prepared for the instability and imbalance that surrounds the toxic combinations that pervaded her. The instability of addiction and mental illness meant that she would always feel alone. I could be holding her with the most loving embrace, whispering my love for her and she would still feel isolated from the entire world. She was hostage to the life she survived, as well as her constantly shifting mental tides. I never saw her first relapse in our home happening in October until it was too late because I couldn't decipher which part had a hold on her: her addiction or her mind.

V

The second week of October a friend of hers from San Diego came to visit. I'd already begun suspecting something was wrong but wanted to wait until after her friend left at the end of the week before confronting her. A few days before her friend had arrived she drove down to San Diego to see her probation officer and didn't return until one in the morning and, when she did come home, she was shaking and evasive, her car was packed with scattered toys for the kids that were open, spread throughout the cabin like a wonton array of pebbles.

She'd been wearing more foundation on her face the night I caught her, and her unease and shaking disposition seized with enough discomfort to shiver the family surrounding her. After dinner, with our children winding down, she disappeared into the bathroom. About an hour passed and I heard the repeated, consistent flicker of her lighter. I'm just lighting incense bellowed from beyond the door.

When her seven-year-old son, dancing for a turn, knocked

at the door she shouted Go away! with a fuming tone and I'd had enough. I opened the door to broad, bewildered eyes and her nude body sitting on the floor, glass pipe in hand. No plan, I packed what I could in a bag, snatched my son, bee-lined out the door of our small home, and pulled out of our driveway. As I was moving through this list of actions she was at my back, at first furious for barging in, then weeping at my silence. Then incensed as I steered down our block. From the rear view I could see her running onto BeJoal Street, hands waving and completely naked. I remember feeling torn be-tween loving her so resolutely and ensuring the safety of my son. I remember trembling as the car inched down the block. I wanted so badly to turn around, leap from the car, and hold her in my arms. I remember knowing that my son had to come first, and I kept going. I was never angry. My heart sim-ply broke as I rounded the corner past the stop sign.

My son and I stayed at a hotel in Lenwood. I'd just been paid and chose a room in the top floor. I just wanted to feel whole and free for the night. I didn't want to think about any-thing except sleep and my son. We sent texts back and forth late into the night, much of it with tears dripping through each letter typed. The next day I got my son to school and, after I'd dropped him off, Jean's mom called to find out what was happening between us after reading some feverish posts on her Facebook page that morning. I didn't tell her much. Before moving to Barstow a few months earlier she'd set me aside to tell me that if anything ever happened with Jean to call her and she'd come and take the twins right away. It would've broken Jean's heart to lose them, so I kept my mouth shut that morning.

Jean called three times shortly after I'd spoken with her mom. On the third ring I answered, and she was crying, incoherent, and her voice drifted in and out of my ear like someone struggling with a whisper. She'd taken the old road

— Route 66 — to Victorville to dose at the clinic, but her car ran out of gas just miles before the interstate. Worried and frantic I rushed across the open highway and found her — and her friend — sitting in the car on the shoulder. She was mumbling and nodding, and her face was smeared damp with sleeplessness and sobs. I called AAA, got the car fueled and followed to her the AM/PM at the interstate entrance. In the course of those few miles she crossed the center line nearly colliding with two or three cars. At the gas station I fueled up her car, emptied her purse of the pipe and bags, and took them both home. At home the first thing she rummaged through was her purse. After a minute of watching her I steadily commented I found your pipe. I tossed it. She was angry and stumbled to the bedroom, striping herself of her clothes. The last image in my mind from that day is her wobbling, exposed frame kneeling on the floor anxiously picking apart the carpet surrounded by a bed of scattered Klonipin.

A month later, with her twins living in at her mothers, she checked herself into Vista Balboa, a crisis house located on Laurel Street, across from Balboa Park in San Diego. A renovated two-story home, the surface atmosphere was community driven and cozy. It was a safe reprieve and the program supported her through a bio-psychosocial approach that emphasized tools to survive and cope. I was hopeful and in love and relieved through our visits. I could see the color in her eyes again and felt the nuzzling thaw of my soul at every embrace. It wasn't the last relapse and it would be her first of two visits to the crisis house within the next year. There were a lot of great days, but the bad ones always came.

VI

There was damage after October. Through that event I shut myself off from her. It wasn't a deliberate callous coldness, but a delicate protection that subconsciously seeped through to the surface. I built a wall around myself for fear of getting hurt by her use and never realized it fully until her death. One of the most tragically helpless feelings is watching the one you love slip away right before your eyes. Beneath those turbulent moments I knew who she was and loved her completely. The feeling is like being forced to lie in bed with the one you love as that person fucks someone else. It's literally torture in its truest form.

But I was always hers. From the first moment we met at my house on Goldfinch in San Diego during the early nineties, to the moment we hugged in the park near her mom's house years later, to this very small, insignificant second as I labor with her memory on a page. I am in love with Jean.

One of the reasons we left San Diego was because her mom was returning from a long trip to South Carolina and simply wanted her house back. The other reason, however, was that her use over that summer had escalated to a degree that required swift action. I confronted her late one night, a week before we packed to move to Barstow together, after I'd come over to be greeted by a home with only her twins. It was two in the morning. The kids were asleep and she was nowhere around the house. When she came walking down the block about thirty minutes later I could see the quiver of her fingers and eyes. Her voice cracked with forced repose, "I was just out for a walk…"

"At two in the morning leaving the twins alone! Your children!"

She retreated to her bathroom as I waited in her room down the hall. I could hear the lighter as seconds ticked and reverberated across the tranquil chaos of wood floors. In her room, door locked, we stood at her disheveled bed surrounded by piles of shoes, boots, and laundry begging for the mercy of a wash. I narrowed to her eyes and asked, "Are you using? I know you are. Just tell me. Please."

Her head lowered faintly, her eyes remained in mine, but her defenses were down. A soft vulnerability supplanted the fight to hide and I could feel love ebbing between us. "Yes", escaped her lips in a soothing, sad melody.

"What?"

"Crack."

"You have to stop, you know that. Do you want to lose us? The twins? me?"

Even she knew it was bad. The money she'd get from me or welfare or social security went to the black or crack before she'd even thought about bills, her car, or the twins. I'd been wiring money from Barstow when I could, but it had already become overwhelming and frightening. She wanted to stop in that moment, but she could not find the strength to simply flush away what she had left. Capturing me in time she bargained. Just let me finish what I have left, and I'm done. I swear.

An apprehensive agreement was reached, and she quickly broke out what she had. Laying her pipe on the night stand she poured the rocks from the small bag and scooped them to the small, charred glass pipe she used. I felt weak and powerless, sobbing through each hit, the smoke flowing across our divide and resting along the edge of moonlight illuminating her room. Once she was done she took my hand, stood up, and slid her summer dress up, over her head revealing her beautiful bare figure. One of the effects of crack is heightened horniness. We were still up when the kids awoke for breakfast the next morning. We hadn't slept.

VII

There were wonderful moments between us that validated and expressed the poetry we shared. Those were gifted times where we knew how lucky we'd been to fall in love with our best friend. As a mother she was vibrant, poised, and radiated her nurturing love to all of our children. She was my backbone and will.

I miss the fondness for feathers; her love of Varo and Goya; the loud cacophony of Jack White, Unwound, The Black Keys, Fugazi, and Circus Lupus; the weakness for Snickers and high heels; her natural flair for arranging flowers; the insatiable appetites; the manic laughter reverberating through the house; little ornate boxes along the windowsills; a glimmer of a tuberose or peony sparkling deep within her hazel eyes; our children weak from her infectious, playful laughter; the way coffee stains littered the kitchen every morning with the joyful rationale of It's not coffee unless it spills!; the way she expertly expressed sultry boots; the array of lingerie she introduced me to… her soft whispers as I slept, the I love you don't ever leave she thought I couldn't hear…the way her hair spilled across my skin…the innate genius of her own writing and the way she wrote herself into my heart. The list is as infinite as the tumultuous fear that commanded her past.

One afternoon, at my son's school, his mother blasted me with accusations of causing our son's flu the week before with a finger on neglect. In the face of a public outburst there's nothing I can do but stand there and take it all. I could feel Jean's fermenting steam rise behind me and the word "cunt" slipped through her lungs. I swiveled around, caught her arm and guided her away and toward our parked car with gentle sternness. After I picked up my son, and the three of us were buckled in, she said "I'm sorry. I just hate her." I nodded my understanding but smiled inside. I was fortunate to have her in my life. She was the voice I couldn't use.

There were hectic mornings, especially when her Jetta was out of the question. She'd have to do the forty-mile drive to the clinic early to get back in time for school. When my son wasn't there I'd walk with the twins and she'd race my car down the street to catch up with our two-block walk. On the days he was with us it'd be a deliberate pace of getting the kids motivated and ready with peanut butter waffles as she sped up the driveway, music screaming, and dust filtering through the kitchen while we ate. Exhausted breath, wide eyes, and Did I tell you today? I love you! for all three kids on the way out the door. And, while the twins were safely living with their grandmother, Jean was mother to mine with a hug and kiss before bed.

Near the end of the fall term my contract with Victor Valley College ended and I was told it wouldn't be renewed for the next term. My heart aching, I texted Jean with the news. At the end of that last shift she was waiting in the parking lot, braving the cold, biting desert winds and standing next to our car. She strolled across the empty lot and, wrapping her arms around me with a kiss. I felt the compassion of her soft voice in my ear. "I'm sorry, baby. It'll be okay. I love you." Back at our house later that night we sat in our small bedroom surrounded by the soft light of candles atop the supple, sadness of our quilted covers. We were talking about how we were going to get through the holidays and the months ahead. "But you don't want me to do "dates", right?"

"What?! No!"

I cried. It was all she thought she knew.

VIII – July 17

We'd planned on moving back to our hometown and getting our own place by August. We left Barstow in June after I'd been commuting to San Diego for two months for work. She was staying with the only person she knew who would put her up, her attorney in Ocean Beach. Staying at my dads with me was out the question because she'd relapsed at his house during the Christmas break. Around the middle of the month, on Father's Day, I sensed something was wrong with her. After several relapses I knew the signs. When she snapped at my son I pulled out of getting a place with her. "You have to be clean for thirty days before I can put you in a home with my son! I need stability for him." It broke my heart to tell her, but I felt I had to protect my son. With what little money I had I paid for her hotel in Hillcrest and hoped for the best. I never stopped loving her and we were still planning a marriage for December.

We spent two hours in her hotel room that Friday before she passed and, as I was I leaving, something about her felt even more off than it had the last few weeks. She mentioned that her mom was picking her up and she'd ducked out of plans with me, something she'd never done before. Later on, after I'd left, I noticed a voicemail from her number. I heard the nervous, high tone of her speech and remained numb for hours. "This is Samantha. I was just returning your call. I'm looking for someone to party with…" Through all her stories I knew that name, and knew that not only was she using, but the life of "dates" had gripped her. When I texted her, it twisted from rigid denial to admission to I'm doing what I need to survive but I'm not doing what you think.

At four in the morning I met her at her hotel. I confronted her with the voicemail and there was nothing left to say after that. Just tears. We held one another on the bed, each of us shaking, sobbing for breath, and desperate for salvation to come. The air was clotted with remorse and heartache. *I didn't know you loved me this much!*

"Of course I love you! I was holding back! I wanted you to get better!"

We made love for the last time that early morning. I can still feel the smooth calm of her skin against mine, her eyes seizing mine and I know, with everything within, we loved one another. But I left, still dazed and held by her in that frame of time. I left feeling shocked and sickened by the thought of her with other men.

Saturday was more texting, phone calls, and *Please! You gotta forgive me.* What I do with those losers and what you and I do aren't nearly the same! to Please come over. I want to say goodbye in person later that evening. The weight of that last text message took several hours to sink in and, when it did, I called and texted paragraphs, pleading with lines of desperation. I called the police twice that night. At four in the morning the officer called my phone to tell me that they couldn't enter her hotel room unless she was actively asking for help. They wouldn't break in unless there was some sign or message that indicated she was asking for assistance. I had none to offer.

At eight in the morning I was pounding on her door. I hadn't slept, and I'd found her ads on Craigslist during the late hours and knew far more than I had the night before. I was desperate, shaking, and sobbing her name with a howl. I frantically needed to know she was safe. All I could do was leave a note. Be Samantha, be Jean… just be mine. Marry me this week and let's fix all of this… The idea to hack her email, and subsequently her Facebook account, came later in the day. Using her account, I posted a message that stated simply *I'm overdosing on heroin. 3942 8th Ave., #15. Please help.* Had I not posted that message she would have been alone in that room for another two days. Still, I was still too late. She'd been gone for four hours when the police finally broke down the door to her room.

An hour after her mother called to tell me she was gone, her voice message from the night before came through. I'm taking every pill in my cupboard. I just got my meds refilled. I'm doing this heroin I have and I'm locking my door. She was always afraid of being alone. In her last moments she only wanted me… she wanted me to come and save her, but I was too late. She didn't want to die alone. I listened to that message every day for months, haunted by my failure to save her.

Through the weeks following I scoured her emails, texts on her phone, and read through her journal, which mostly consisted of me and her love and worry about my own stress. She wanted to show me she could stand on her own and be a real partner but was terrified I'd find out about that path she took to get there. I saw her every day during weeks prior to her death and she cried herself to sleep every night after I left. I know how much she loved me and how much she felt unworthy of my faith. If she'd only seen in herself the rippling exquisiteness I always saw.

I discovered voice to text messages under her Google archive and heard her speaking to her connect as far back as February and read how other dealers and her pimp were aiding her. I came to know how much life they robbed of her through drugs and abuse, pushing her over a precipice she both dreaded and couldn't escape from. I learned about the rape on her birthday. I found the pictures she used for the ads on her computer and knew that E. Wynn took them that same night. I emailed him if, for nothing else, to ensure that it sunk in that I knew, and he took her life as surely as the sex trade and all the dangers that came with it. And I learned that the "dates" began in May, before we moved back to San Diego. I never should have taken a job away from her, leaving her alone.

She took her life because she thought she'd lost me for good, but that was never true. I never left, and I always understood. I knew why she paced whenever we were thick within crowds and why she rocked in her chair two hours after dosing. I knew why she counted and why she needed a cigarette whenever she spied a certain type of man. I knew, I understood, and I loved her. Others have told me that I probably gave her an extra year of life. It's a dear thought, but not a comfort as my hand absent-mindedly reaches for hers in the car realizing it'll never feel the fold of her fingers again.

And many friends we share have expressed their thoughts encompassing her addiction and suicide, calling it a "choice". I understand the notion. I even agree with the view to some degree. For some who deal with an addiction it tapers down to a choice between the drug and the people in your life. For me, the choice to remain sober has become a simple matter of daily practice. But to label such acts as a "choice" for everyone who's held by this disease is a faulty premise. For Jean the addiction wasn't a choice. It was more than compulsion or urge. It was a design of temptation commanded by abusive men, an unhealthy, ravenous sex drive, and a brew of mental illnesses that was beyond her control or ability to manage. In a very real sense she was attacked by herself and the world around her at the same time every second of her life. For Jean, "Samantha" wasn't just an alter ego. She was as real as Deborah Jean Gadzala, allowing her to confront the chaos she dove into for nearly ten years. Samantha was that half of her mind she fought to bury in vain because it was a terrifying part of who she was.

Her grace and poise lie within her yearning to strive for a better life for herself and our children. In the end that mélange within her mind attached to addictions that couldn't be overcome. She never had a choice. She was imprisoned all along and throughout her life.

This is where I'm at. I'm still falling in love with the richness of the person I love, turmoil and all. She was ever a brewing, broiling storm on the verge of a colored array of moods and universes. I survive each day knowing how miserably I failed her and how much I missed. My days are seeded with should haves and why didn't I see? The very moment I feared the worst, desperate in front her hotel door, whatever barrier I'd built to combat the pain of her addiction simply crumbled, as if I were suddenly allowed to feel the full measure of all my love for her. Every day the pain of never being able to share the vastness of that love with her kills me just a little bit more. The moment I learned her body had been found remains fixed within my heart, as if a permanent portrait of wailing pain. It was as if the air around me had been washed away.

Two days after she died I had a court hearing over my son. I was awarded primary custody. I would not have him here with me if not for her. It's a bittersweet victory, at best. All I have now is this gift she gave me.

I love you, Jean. Always.

Elephant

It's an ornate elephant necklace
with a brunette hue, ordained
with dollops of sprinkled flowers
and deep, dark orange petals
…or is it a pink. It's tanned
and aged, like the chain that
holds it free as I hang this connection
to your life, the speechless seconds
locked within a nearby picture of you,
standing within the edge of our
old doorway. Your sunglasses
hang at the tip of your nose, and
you eye the camera with a poised,
poesy prose. You seem to peer your gaze
through the lens to this moment

as I hang this chain that
must of have enjoyed aligning
the nape of your neck, with freedom
and a sultry solidarity that was meant
for the adjusted daily life between us.

Survivor's Guilt

There are many debilitating conditions that can rob you of who you truly are without it being anything substantially medical. Survivor's guilt is one of the worst. Sleep becomes a challenge and the pillow seems like a bitter enemy. It scratches at your day as you struggle with each motion of speech or action. In the face of others, you learn how to compartmentalize. On the inside, you're simply falling apart, cherry picking the world for meaning or forgiveness. On July 16, 2016, I learned that not only was the woman I love using heroin again, but she was posting photos for "dates". She'd gone back into prostitution.

Jean, through her deteriorating mindset, had called my phone as "Samantha", leaving a message for potential client. I'd already learned of her drug use and paid for a residential hotel she was staying in. I did this protect my son. There is no guilt with that choice and, while that took time to develop, I feel it was the right thing to do. I needed to protect my son from the instability and mood swings that would express themselves through her addiction and borderline personality disorder.

San Diego can be humid, hot, and unforgiving during the summer months and, as I drove west on the 94 freeway toward her hotel I could feel those swells as my heart broke. I found a place to park on Eighth Avenue, stepped out of my car with my eyes fixed on the ground, and dialed her number.

"I'm here. Come down and open the door."

"What's wrong?" she asked. She could hear the devastation in my mood.

"Just come down." I started to cry. The strangest thing about that moment is that I'd already forgiven her.

I stood at the foot of the stairs to the hotel, drenched with sweat from the heat and sobbing at the thought of her with other men. She opened the door and I walked up the stairs. Before I crossed the threshold, she held me close with every ounce of heart and song.

"What's going on?"

"Can we just go upstairs to your room first?"

"Of course, honey. I love you"

My response crackled with "I love you too."

She was stunning. She wore a white Summer dress that allowed a vague peek at what was beneath. Her perfume wafted through air, as if to defy the pot smoke that permeated the halls. My mind was breaking, and time was both frozen and moving.

Once we got to her room she turned and kissed me.

"What is wrong?"

Sobbing, I pulled my phone from my pocket and fumbled with the keys and the screen to find the voicemail she'd left earlier. As soon as she heard the Hi, this is Samantha her poise and grace slipped toward a white, ashen sheen. She was now crying with me.

"Oh God!" she cried.

"How long!" I shouted.

She fumbled for a moment, struck by both my outburst and knowledge that I now knew. There was nowhere for her to hide. "Since July 4th," her voice crackling an air similar to my own. "I didn't know you felt this strongly. I thought you put me in this hotel because things were going to end."

I held her hand and looked into the impressionistic hazel

eyes that had always baffled me with sheer happiness. "I paid for the hotel room because of your addiction. I got you this place because I needed to protect my son, and I'd hoped you find your way to rehab. I love you, Jean."

"Oh God! I love you too, baby."

She held me close. She wiped my tears away attempting to assuage the monster that stood between us. Her hands roamed as she kissed me with depth and passion. She took an inch backward to undo my belt buckle. I was hanging by a thread and, with my back against the wall, we made love. I didn't know it'd be for the last time. Before I left, I told her, "I love you, Jean. I still want to be married by December. Just hold on."

"I love you too," she cried.

As I walked down the stairs to toward the front door of the hotel, I couldn't shake the betrayal. All of those men. Jean had told me stories about her past. Some men found pleasure in punching, while others simply wanted to rape her. She suffered all those moments for her addiction. How far would it take her this time?

Later that evening, after I'd gotten home, I received a text message from her. *I love you. I need you to come over so I can say goodbye in person.* The weight of her message didn't sink in right away. At first glance, I thought she was breaking up with me out of remorse. By the time the message garnered the heft of the rhetoric it carried it was 11 p.m. I called the San Diego police department to do a well check on her. I was frantic. I was falling apart.

I couldn't sleep, and I just needed to know how far things had gotten. I hacked her email account and then her Facebook account. I read through secretive messages from her dealer and a few messages from customers who'd tracked her down using her phone number. I also found another email account, sammywillplease@gmail.com. Under that account I found her Craigslist postings and emails spanning back two months. She'd lied about how long she'd been seeing men for money. There was a mixture of treacherous duplicity and the pain of realizing how far gone she truly was.

At four in the morning I called San Diego police to do another well-person check since I hadn't heard anything about the first. Twenty minutes later the officer called to tell me that she wasn't answering the door and, unless there was a definitive cry for help, there was nothing he could do. The text message wasn't enough. I was helpless. I was numb.

The next morning, I waited at the foot of the stairs of the hotel. As soon as someone came out I rushed through the doorway and up the stairs to her room. I knocked and knocked with no answer. I tried to open the door, but it was locked. I wrote a note telling her I'd marry that week. I just needed to know she was okay. It was all I thought I could do at that moment. I needed to be in Hesperia that evening to pick up my son from his mom. I called a friend of mine, Steve, and asked him if he'd mind driving because I hadn't slept. I just knew something was terribly wrong with Jean.

Steve and I had to leave by 2pm to make it to Hesperia to pick up my son. Just before we left I got the idea to post to her account as her. I logged into her Facebook account and typed: I am overdosing on heroin. Please help! I followed that up with the address and room number. The outpouring of our friends who'd stepped up and called the police was incredible. About an hour before reaching Hesperia I received a voicemail that she'd sent the night before. She must've shut her phone off hoping I'd rush over. "I'm taking every pill I have. I just got my meds refilled. I'm taking this heroin I have and I'm locking my door. I love you." Soon after that her mother called. The authorities had found her lifeless body. She had been dead for over four hours. My entire world screamed and stopped. I couldn't breathe through the tears.

Half my world was torn apart. I lost my love and future. The blinding anguish was unbearable. She had been alive when I was knocking at her door and I all did was leave a fucking note and post a Facebook message an hour too late. I had failed her.

All I wanted was a bullet in my head to join her. She hated being alone. This is my guilt, that feeling that I should have done more. Time doesn't heal this wound. This is my constant memory replayed over and over with misery. Broken sounds shake me awake each night and my heart sinks as I know she's not there anymore. Each night I simply fall through holes and feel my mind breaking. I miss her and it's all I know. This is my pain. This is what I live with each day. A guilt as deep as a mine shaft.

The Stone Steps

I remember you
as I scrub the coffee stains
from the floor, listening
to some vivid, faraway
morning happiness captured
by that ritual in your voice.

"It's not coffee unless it spills."

I remember you in a periphery
of cream-lined Pacific tides
with their sharp, lyrical roar.

Dusted memories shimmer
with profane, glittering
emptiness, as stars shed
their tears across an array
of fractioned, forlorn
porcelain seconds, aching
for the dreamlike embrace
of your folded arms.

I remember you
as I polish the grounds
of an entire swirling globe.

Aftermath

|

There are only two deaths that no one should ever experience. The first is the death of a child. The age doesn't matter. It's against the balance of life for one's child to perish before the parent. The second is the death of someone you're in love with. This second one may lighten in it's sting through old age, but to lose someone so close in the middle of life is sheer hell. If I were forced to describe it the closest description would be that it's akin to losing your own soul. No pain is more profound or painful than losses such as these.

The moment I learned of Jean's death I cried out with such an awful, chilling call that the driver — my friend Steve — could feel shivers from the scream within the car we were in. The reality hit me with the strength and impact of a steam engine. I felt my soul rip in half as the moment around me froze. Passing cars seemed to inch by while my world crumbled to the floor. The desert mountains seemed calculated and measured through the length of my wailing and a vast pain that spread across the dusty terrain.

We were a half hour from picking up my son in Hesperia. Steve did the best he could to console my wound, but the bitter, gnashing of pain was too much to allow for any comfort. I'd asked him to drive that day because I hadn't slept the night before. Somehow, I knew there was something wrong with Jean. That morning — before we left — I slipped a note under her doorway letting her know that I'd marry her that week and we'd get help. Anything she wanted so I long as she was okay. She was still breathing with a soft, slight beating heart when I was there. For months I would admonish myself for not kicking the door in to save her.

Desert mountains, bare and rocky, seemed to augment the slow, seeping moments within the cab of the car. Seconds were painfully long, and my tears refused to cease their waterfall. Yet time stood still at the shock of her death. She would no longer spill coffee with me nearby to clean it up. She would no longer chastise me for not taking better care of myself. My room would no longer welcome some new statue or necklace of an elephant. Her beaded jewelry would all but collect dust along the fractured lines of my heart. Her eyes would never gaze into mine knowing the love we shared. Through the suction of immense anguish I realized that I would have to explain this to my son very soon.

We were early to the Starbucks, where we were meeting with my son's mom. My face was coated in tortured signs of tears and the hurting of a running nose that comes with crying so fiercely. I barely knew my surroundings, but I found a shirt in the back seat of the car and used that to wipe my face and blow my nose. It's likely I soaked the shirt with my grief. The wind was blowing hard in Hesperia that evening when my son's mom finally pulled into the parking lot. I pulled her aside first before speaking with Dylan. In my mind such news should come from both his parents and I wasn't equipped to handle this on my own. Dylan and Jean had been close.

My own voice was barely audible beneath the howl of the wind and the screams in my own soul.

"What happened?" she asked. It was obvious a tragedy had taken place.

"Jean's dead. I'd put her in a residential hotel because she began using heroin again. I couldn't have Dylan around that. They found her body an hour ago," I explained with shaking heartache.

"Oh my God! I'm glad it's not your dad. That's what I thought at first. I'm sorry," she said as she offered me a surprising hug. We hated one another so, for her to offer an embrace, crafted a humanizing moment between us that extended beyond the differences that divide. For a moment we were just parents.

The two of us walked toward Dylan, who was standing against his mother's car waiting for me. My face was wet, and my entire body shivered with shock. My cheeks were wet, and the suffering shined in my eyes. I couldn't hide my emotions from him and my voice shook.

"Dylan… Jean's dead, son," I said. He was frozen and quiet. "Do you understand what that means?"

"Yes. Is that why you're crying?" he asked.

"Yes. Daddy's very sad." And he hugged me… I didn't want to let go of him.

Dylan never cried through the trip back to San Diego. Every so often he'd reach forward from his seat behind me, put his hand on my neck and say "I love you" as I continued to shiver and shed tears. I would find out months later that he didn't want to cry because I was already too sad, and I needed him. I love my son.

$$||$$

The week of Jean's death was sharply the most painful time of my entire life. My love — my reason and partner — was dead. Moreover, I had a custody hearing in Victorville two days after her death. Months before she'd pushed me to file for full custody of Dylan after learning just how much time his mother had kept him out of school trying to prove he had cerebral palsy. Additionally, I'd get stories about his mom getting mad at him for breaking her pipe or losing the remote control to the television. The stories were heartbreaking, and Jean felt that I would be the better parent to have him through the week. I'd never gotten him to school late and always made sure he was fed, homework done, and loved. So, at her goading, I filed for custody.

I left Dylan with an old friend for the night as I made my way to Barstow to be closer to where the hearing was being held the next morning. It was a long and lonely drive as visions of us were etched along each mile. I pulled up to the house that Jean and I had shared over the past year (I was still paying rent on it in case the hearing went awry) and just sat in the driveway. It was around 11pm and the lights were on. I'd asked an acquaintance, Ally, to watch the house with her boyfriend while Jean and I were in San Diego.

As I sat there in the driveway dreading the thought of entering a home we'd shared a truck pulled in behind my car. It was then that the front door opened, and Ally and her boyfriend were carrying Jean's dresser outside. I got out of my car angered.

"What the fuck are you doing?" I asked.

"We sold the dresser to Mike," said Ally. "I thought you wanted the furniture gone."

"She JUST died!"

"So, do you want us to put it back and give Mike back his money?"

They were tweakers and poor. Jean had warned me not to let them watch our house, but I knew very few people in Barstow. Feeling defeated I said, "No. Just get it over with."

As they continued to the load Mike's truck with Jean's dresser, I walked inside and was immediately stung by the scene within. Her clothes lined the wall inside garbage bags and the boxes she'd packed months before sat in the far corner of the living room. I dropped to my knees in front of one of the bags of clothes and just spilled to tears. She was gone, but I could feel her ghost throughout the tiny home. I knew that — no matter the outcome of the custody hearing — there was no way I could ever live in this house again. The pain would be too much for me endure. I crumbled before what was left of her and that enveloped me, as if some painful blanket had been wrapped around me a shroud.

I slept in the kid's old room that night. Actually, it's more apt to say that I took several Ambien to pass out that night. In the morning I took a shower and did my best to get ready for the court hearing. I was still in shock and crying. I left the house and stopped for gas at a truck stop in Lenwood. There wasn't much left on my card, but the pump allowed me to fill up the tank. It sounds strange, but I felt her that morning. I rummaged through my backpack for Vicodin. My back was killing me, and I had the hearing and a long drive that day. It was then that I realized that either Ally or her boyfriend had robbed me of my pain pills. Fucking tweakers!

III

I couldn't stop sobbing at the courthouse. It's fair to say that I sobbed and wept for months after Jean's death, but it was most profound that day with the added pressure of how my custody hearing would turn out. As I entered the courthouse I was followed by Dylan's mother. We never spoke before a hearing, however, in the hallway before being called into court she said: "You should probably ask for a continuance considering what you're going through." I was inclined to agree until we were all called into the courtroom itself. When I received my copy of the mediator's report I quickly learned that primary physical custody would be awarded to me thanks to Jean. His mother knew this when she spoke to me in the hallway.

Something about the tenor of that day has always struck me. It's as if, through the veil of death, Jean had somehow been watching over me. At least, that's how it felt. From the moment I was able to get gas to the custody hearing I truly thought I felt her arms around me somehow. The drive back to San Diego was long, but somehow calm in her thoughts. I remembered long drives and lazy afternoons watching Outlander. As the speedometer held I could feel the tips of her fingers lightly caressing that core at the back of my neck. She was a part of me that day, so much so that I could almost hold her hand as I drove back to the city to pick up Dylan. Something about that particular day held a certain magic.

IV

The rest of the week didn't offer the same, calm melancholy as Tuesday. The rest of the week was fueled by pinpricked realizations that she was gone and never coming back. It was as if love carried with it a kind of immense pain with nowhere to siphon or ease the tension. I wept and bawled. I felt the fusion of loss and agony of being alive without her hand in mine. Dylan was my only solace from so much turmoil. Had my son not been at my side that week I would have surely followed Jean in death.

Knowledge can be one of most beneficial components of everyday living. The more one knows the more one is aware of their surroundings and the world beyond. However, knowledge is not always the feast that one expects. Here is what I knew: I knew that Jean took her own life because I'd learned of her prostitution and the scope of her drug use. While those who knew her peripherally assumed her death a tragic overdose, I knew different. I knew this because her last communiques were to me and they were pleading. I was living with the guilt of doing nothing. I was living with the guilt of not knowing how to digest all I'd learned, but I never had time to tell her I loved and forgave her without question.

The day after the hearing I was at her mother's house. They'd cleared out Jean's hotel room the day prior and were going through her things. Her mother asked me to help with scanning pictures for the services, which were to be held that Saturday. As she was going through her things, she pulled out a man's bag and sweatshirt and showed them to me.

"Are these yours?"

"No," I hesitated. Then the realization of who those clothes belonged to — E. Wynn — bombarded me like an unfeeling blunt instrument. This was the man who'd taken the pictures she'd used to sell herself online. I shivered and repeated, "No, no, no…!" and fell into agonizing cry as the flood of all she must have suffered gripped me. I longed to be with her. I was immediately plunged into pieces at the sight of another man's clothes.

"Okay. These go in the trash," said her mother. She embraced me from behind. She was stronger than I was considering her daughter's death. Jean had a lengthy of history of addiction and mental disorder. In her mother's mind it was just a matter of time before Jean's death would be realized. She had been expecting this outcome, but I had not.

Without her my life was an unvarnished, merciless war of inner conflict. I was stained by the centers of guilt and loss so intense that the necessities of everyday life — food, sleep, and natural self-care — were aspects slipping from my grasp of sanity. Within that week I lost nearly ten pounds alone and desperately needed friends who already had lives of their own and not much time for my turmoil. I felt alone and needed someone to just hold my hand through the horror.

V

Social media can be a wonderful way to keep in touch with those who live faraway. It can even be a pulpit for change or discussion. Looking at her page I read the comments, some damning me for not doing enough for her while alive, and others saddened by the loss of yet another friend to accidental overdose. In my saddened passion I felt that everyone needed to know the truth of her death. That it was not an accidental overdose, but one of intent because she thought she'd lost my love. I wrote a long, fervent post regarding the last day of her life. I told of how helpless I felt when the police wouldn't enter her room simply because she wasn't asking for help. I explained how I'd hacked her account and used it post a faux plea from her for help. This was the only way the police would enter her room. By the time they entered, however, she'd been dead for nearly four hours.

The post didn't stay up long, and some were angered at me for writing about her last days. I received death threats against my life by those she called friends. I took the post down after a few hours and it was probably too soon for such a frank dissertation. Or, perhaps, people simply needed to remember her in their own way and without the fluttering truth that I knew. In my pain I'd forgotten that people are allowed to remember the dead with whatever light comforts them. The truth doesn't matter.

The threats and blame I received sunk into me and molded an ever more saddened state of mind. Dylan was a comfort, but the reality of everyone's virtual viciousness toward me took a toll. I lost sleep and more weight. I became unhinged and craved the appointment of dying with Jean. In life she couldn't stand to be alone. In death, I felt I could not leave her by herself. In my mind, she still needed me to fill the gates of that solitude.

Two days before her services her body was released for cremation. Jean's mother saw her daughter lying peacefully on death's table and took a picture to show me. When I saw it I simply broke. In death she'd somehow found a way to look peaceful in sleep. I could almost reach through to wake her. Through her experiences of abuse as a prostitute she never slept soundly. No matter how gently I'd tried to nudge to awaken she'd startle at the merest touch. She was used to brutality and being awoken with harsh rousing. This picture of her on her death bed offered some peace from those butchering men and I cried.

VI

Somehow, I made it to Saturday and the services for her. A few of my friends showed up to support me. I was afraid of the threatened backlash from social media and needed the relief of a few good friends. By this time, I'd retrieved her phone from her mother (which was technically mine) and learned a little more about the last days of her life. A man called a day before and, using her street name, left an implored message: "Sammy, Sammy, Sammy. I've got a 140 and a ripe dildo for your tight pussy. Call me Sammy. 140!" Hearing this message made me sick and faint. It's not easy to digest that the woman you love had to resort to prostitution in order to fund her addiction.

Along with that message I received threats upon my own life. These were people who'd supported her addiction in her final days in one way or another. These were people that knew she was prostituting in order to survive. These people threatened to show up at her services in order to beat me to death. Afraid for both myself and my son, the services carried a certain frailty that's hard to explain. I needed to surround myself with friends who would have my back should something actually occur. Thankfully the services were peaceful and allowed some semblance of release for myself and her family. She was never truly a Christian but had sought the spirituality of some higher power through the years, understanding that recovery from addiction required such an overflowing resignation. Despite her efforts, she never found that calm.

My son was with me that day and, as the adults grieved, the children played in the parking lot, resilient of the loss. I was almost jealous of their ability to simply be children and find enjoyment. All that consumed me was her loss and I spent that day half sobbing and half breaking down but trying desperately to be a parent. I hadn't slept for several days and the next day I would have to drive him to Hesperia to drop him off with his mother. Perhaps, I thought, I could find some way to pull myself together while he was away that week.

The day after I'd dropped him off I admitted myself into a mental ward. I'd gone days without sleep and the pain of missing Jean pushed my thoughts toward dire thoughts of joining her, so she wouldn't be alone in death. I needed sleep and calm. The ward was small, and the residents weren't too bad in terms of mental impediments. Therapy, coupled with the medication they gave me for sleep, seemed to ease my break down.

VII

After my release I contacted Jean's mother. I spent a lot of time with her and the twins during those initial weeks. We went through her belongings from the hotel. The computer she was using was also mine, so I took that with me to my dad's house in Chula Vista. Logging into the computer I was desperate for answers of some sort. What I found was probably more than anyone should know regarding the death of a loved one. I found hundreds of pictures of her nude or in lingerie, posing for ads on Craigslist so she could earn the money she needed for the hotel, heroin, and crack. The photos were both alluring and painful. Painful because they were never meant for me. They were meant for other men.

I also found her accounts on sugar daddy sites and emails she'd long forgotten. In all, I uncovered roughly ten email accounts spanning back five years. I got a roughly hewn portrait of the disease she suffered. She'd go months on the mend, free of drugs and determined to be a mother to her children and then, as if in an instant, the addiction and borderline personality disorder would take control. A pattern emerged as I sifted through each email and ad she'd posted. I began to understand fully the catastrophe that was her mind. It would be months before I could accept that, had she not succeeded in her suicide attempt that July, she most certainly would have accomplished that goal eventually and there was nothing I could do to stop it.

For a brief time, I saw her therapist in El Cajon. After I revealed who I was and what had happened to Jean, he gave me a test. The test was intended for borderline personality disorder and depression. What I learned from that test was that she was at the far end of the negative spectrum in every way. No amount of medication or therapy would have offered her a "cure". Her malady was terminal. In time I had to capitulate to the truth. No matter how much I loved her, she would have eventually died before our lives could unfold together.

Her computer also revealed the journal she kept. I learned when the last relapse began, how desperate she was that I wouldn't find out, and how much she loved me. I learned about the twin's father and how he supplied her with crack. I learned that her old pimp had been supplying her with heroin, and I learned how many people knew. From her phone I learned she'd been raped by E. Wynn, the homeless friend who'd taken all of the photos I'd found on her computer. An older email revealed that her attorney, R. Burns, extorted her for sex as payment for his services. I learned how she got her drugs both in San Diego and Barstow and from whom. I learned more than I needed. Through it all she didn't want to lose me.

VIII

I had access to her phone. It was under my account, so recovering the texts and numbers wasn't a problem. I'm an alcoholic by nature, which makes me obsessive. I needed to know what she did with these men. I wanted to know when she met with them and what went on. I posed as her and contacted nearly forty men promising a discount if they'd recall what they did with her. Men replied back with an eagerness and willingness that I found both astonishing and disgusting.

I read one of her posted ads and texts:

Hi, I'm Sammi, an adventurous milf and party girl who loves to fuck and suck orally talented, tight shaved pussy. I'm willing to do the girlfriend experience but I don't do Greek. Discreet drama, drug and disease free. I have transportation so I'm willing to travel you must cover gas costs. Please, serious inquiries only.

One of her text messages to a client read:

I'm looking for company. I'm headed out to eat right now but am available all night. I do get a donation for my time and I hate how grasping that sounds. It is what it is. I like to give, but I also love to have straight up, no-holds-barred sex. It depends on my partner and the mood. I'll be back at the room around 7:30—8:00 pm. My phone number is 619-646-7005.

One customer got back to me, thinking he was texting her, and revealed:

Hello Samantha, we did have business. (More than once) I came in and you took me to the back room by the bathroom. I got undressed and sat on the edge of the bed. You got down on your knees and sucked my cock like the bj-queen that you are. After sucking my cock, you got up on the bed and laid on your back. I got on top and slide my cock in but the condom broke, so I attempted to finish by jacking off.
The last it was 80.
I have seen you more than once. The last time I believe was during the day. I came over and you took me to the back room. I got undressed and sat on the edge of the bed. You got on your knees and began to suck my cock. "Which you do very well" I then laid you on your back and started getting busy when the condom broke. Had to finish by jacking off while you fingered your pussy

O yes, the first was late at night and I was kinda tired. I came over you took me to the back room I got undressed and you dropped to your knees and begin to suck my cock. Moved to edge of bed where you continued to suck my cock. You asked what I wanted next and I said: up to you. So, you bent over I slid in my cock hitting it from behind. From there you laid on your back, but I was too tired to get a nut so we ended it there

This particular encounter would have coincided with my son being in the home during their transaction. The knowledge of that was revolting and I will owe my son an amends for years to come for putting him in danger.

I began placing times and days together. I remember how, when I'd come to see her at the residential hotel, she'd be fresh from a shower and now I knew why. She wanted to clean the stain of the last customer from herself before interacting with me.

Another customer texted back with this event from San Diego:

Our encounter was naughty. I know we were both turned on by each other. You sat me on the bed and devoured my cock and was slurping on it. We were both getting really hot. I had to return the favor. After seeing your sexy ass, I had to lay you down for some oral. After a short time licking your clit and your tasty little ass you came so good. You said that's the first time you came from oral I was rock hard and had to enter you. Did missionary for a bit and then you wanted me to bend u over. Oooo that was fantastic. Fucking u from behind and looking at that sweet ass.

The messages I received were vile and nauseating:

Yea I remember. You're beautiful as always. You gave me best Bj ever and I got to cum all over u. Omg nice I gotta see that pussy and tits again. MILF for sure. I had u wearing fishnets. I remember you tasted so sweet Those eyes looking up at me while my cock was in ur mouth telling me u want it inside u. Then u riding me till I creampied your beautiful pussy full of my seed Omg that pussy and ass I could eat ur pussy all day I think it was night time, but I am not a 100 percent positive. Yup you gave me the best bbbj and cream pie ever. I am Italian you said my dick was one of the best you had.

Another wrote back with:

When you sucked my dick. That really made it throb and made me want to pop and when you got on top of me your pussy felt so wet and warm. You were super nasty. I don't remember what you were wearing.

I had to park one block over because there wasn't any parking, when u Came to the door we went upstairs to the left to get to your room. It may have been that time of month for? If I'm not mistaken I loved the head.

One customer she met both in our home in Lenwood and at the hotel in San Diego:

We did bareback and I creampied your pussy.

I loved how your pussy tasted and how hard your little clit got as I sucked and licked it, you go so wet as I inserted my finger into your pussy while still licking and sucking you

I started to massage your g spot with my fingers while licking harder on you enlarged clit

You started arching your back and grinding your pussy into my face, harder and harder I could feel you were about to cum and I licked and sucked harder to get you over the top. With a few more grinds of your pussy into my face, I could feel your vagina spasm orgasmicaly.

I was almost ready to explode but wanted my hot cum deep in your wet pussy You spread those pussy lips and slide me full length deep into your love box. The feeling was intense. You started grinding yourself and those hips into my crouch.

Each grind and stroke massaging my hard member, closer and closer to its explosion crescendo. Finally, with one deep thrust, of your hips I hit Nirvana. Pumping the full contents of my balls deep into your hungry pussy I could feel your vagina milking every drop of my man juice, like a thirsty desert traveler drinking from his canteen

Your pussy continued to spasm and I was starting to get hard again

I pushed you on the bed, as my cock withdrew from your pussy, some of my batter started to drip out

I put you on all fours and proceeded to fuck you hard and deep I could see my cock plunging in and out of your little pussy, cum was trying to escape from your love box, I wanted every drop inside you again

I continued to pound your pussy till I felt the cum rising again in my shaft, with one great thrust, I penetrated you deeply pumping one last batch of my man juice into the deepest reaches of your being We both collapsed onto the bed, in a pool of cum and sweat.

I read over forty texts and emails from men who'd been with her within a span of weeks. I learned about men she'd been with years prior through her older emails. Don Baldwin was a regular she'd made the most money from. He wrote back via email with:

We met at Burt's twice and then spent a few days at my mountain cabin. Then you returned to your mom's place above the canyon. We met there several times as well as a little park on the other side of the canyon toward the ocean.

I went with you several times to enroll in Mesa College. I dropped you off a few times at a church north on Genesse.

We visited the area off Poinsettia where your two older kids lived. We also met them at a park where you were allowed to visit them with a women chaperone.

We also visited Trinidad at his 2bs floor apartment off 54th Street. This was around the time he got you pregnant.

I took you to get suboxin (sp?) on Friars Road several times.

I visited you at Sharps Hospital when you delivered twins. I loaned you my laptop at the hospital and you had your girlfriend return it to me saying you could no longer see me.

Later we met, and I paid for you and your girlfriend to live in an apartment a mile South-West of your mom's. You treated me like shit so, after you had druggies stay with you I had move you out!

We met at a motel at the East end on motel circle south twice. On of those times you brought a girlfriend who lived around 4th and El Cajon Blvd.

We would have dinner &/or breakfast at the motel diner.

After that we drifted apart?

The last time I remember seeing you was when we took your 1yr old twins to the park. Don't worry about how you treated me, you were on drugs most of the time!

When we were out and about you were good company. I was pleased to spend time with you.

Naked was your best outfit and I did like your pussy; Especially up close and personal.

We used both her room and your downstairs room.

Eating pussy was nice!

It was exciting anyplace!

Jean had two pimps during her years on the streets: KennyBoy and Burt. Burt was the father of her twins. During her final weeks alive he was supplying her with crack and robbed her of almost $800. KennyBoy was ensuring she was getting the heroin she needed and sleeping with him to make up the difference. She'd meet with him before and after I'd left the hotel… and I never suspected.

Reading through all the texts and emails that men sent back after she died I began to despise the role of men in women's lives. Almost any man I saw seemed to fit the profile of the men she'd slept with for money. Some were married with children and had to make discreet arrangements to meet with her. Others were just junkies who had just enough to pay about eighty bucks for whatever they wanted. Others would pay her in meth and money. Her illness was pervasive and dangerous during those last weeks, and I learned — after reading their texts — that I kind of hated men. Even her attorney took advantage of her. I also learned E. Wynn had raped her — on her birthday.

IX

I loved Jean. I still love her. I love the person I knew buried beneath the hardened years on the streets suffering through broken bones, rape, and absolute humiliation. She was strong for surviving all she had, and I respected her for that. She used to watch these horrendous videos of jigger removals and rotting flesh on YouTube. She'd show me what she was watching, but it was too gruesome even for me to stomach. One day I figured why those videos fascinated her. They were the only things worse than what she'd suffered through the years. I spent ten minutes watching videos with her upon that realization, kissed on the forehead, and simply said "I love you."

I spent months weeping in anguish at her loss. It took months for me to become angry at her for putting my son in a situation that was not just disgusting, but dangerous. When I cleared out our little home in Lenwood I learned the full scope of her addiction. I found three pipes, four baggies of meth, and pills she'd hidden in boots and small boxes. She could never walk away from her addiction entirely and it gripped her. Her addiction fueled her borderline personality disorder and allowed Samantha to do the things that Jean could not in order to keep her addiction funded.

Through all of that knowledge I still remain hers. I loved her dearly, and parts of me still do. Her pictures and clothing are packed away in the closet of my new home — one where her ghost doesn't invade my dreams as much.

There is still one nightmare I have on occasion. When I have this one, I wake up and getting back to sleep is near impossible. In this dream she's dressed in the clothes she died in — jeans, black shirt, and my favorite pink scarf. She's barely breathing, but still waiting for me to save her. I'm above her in the tiny hotel room, helpless as I listen to my pounding on the door beyond. I float there watching her take her last breath. At her last gasp I awake, barely able to breath myself and knowing I won't be getting back to sleep.

What It's Like Now

For a time, I had pictures of Jean hanging on the walls of this new house. There were two that were pinned to either side of this desk I write from so that I could look up, see her face, and drift off into some bubble where she's alive and the memories don't attack. They're gone now and not because I've forgotten her or felt a need to move on. She will remain a part of who I am for years to come. I loved her deeply and a part of who I am today is forged by knowing her. Her pictures and belongings are hidden so that my son can move on and so that I can find some healthy solace with her memory.

For a long time, her memory and the loss of her in my life was an aggressive cancer that spread throughout my day-to-day life. I tried grief groups and church, but nothing seemed to ease the ache I felt of losing her. In grief groups I felt like an outcast. Most had lost loved ones to old age or illness. It seemed I was the only one who'd lost someone to the grips of addiction of mental illness. I felt alone.

What's truly miraculous was that I didn't drink through her death. Somehow, I intuitively knew that to drink would not ease the loss, that after a night of drinking she'd still be dead and I'd be alone, so what was the point in that? Moreover, I wanted to ensure that all I felt was real. That my anguish and fluid, tender sorrow born of my love for her was something true and material.

I did find a social media group specific to those who'd lost loved ones to addiction. Heroin is the most prevalent of all the deaths as far as I can tell. It allowed me to vent and shed my tears online without bothering friends. Your friends are there for you for a time but, soon, they have lives to run back to and whatever your problems are become more a nuisance than anything else.

After I'd packed away her portraits and clothes, I was comfortable with the notion of raising my son alone. As I write this, I have my son most of the time and his mother is without a home to live in after being evicted from section eight housing. While I'm sure she's doing her utmost to find a home, she's living out of her car and it concerns me when I have to drop off Dylan with her.

I'd grown accustomed to the idea of being alone, with only my son for company and love. We have our own small little family. I admit it gets a little confusing at times. Being a single father to a little boy is something unique. He's not just my son and I'm not just his parent. In some ways we're roommates living in a bachelor pad. You can tell it's a boy's residences with the lack of foliage, video games in front of the television, and toys riddled here and there on the floor.

Jean remains a fixture in my heart. She always will. We shared a youth and an adulthood…and we shared a love like no other. Her music survives in corners of my dreams. But if I had to be honest about her state of mind she would have died eventually whether we married or not. That's not an easy admission, but it's the truth. Jean suffered from border-line personality disorder. She was a cutter when she thought she'd done something wrong. Her mental illness was as pronounced and severe as her addiction. One of the things I never understood was why both were treated separately, rather than together. In my mind, it makes more sense to treat both conditions simultaneously because one feeds upon the other.

Jean was a lover of elephants and medium roast coffee, which she spilled every time. She was a mother and could be a nurturing soul to all those who knew her well. She appreciated the painted arts and loved punk rock almost as much as I do, though she hated the classics. She is ever etched in my heart and will most likely sneak heavily into my dreams for as long as I live. In many ways we will always belong to one another. In other ways I'm looking forward to discovering what's new.

I Blame Her

Your left leg is propped forward
as I remember all the men who
participated in your death and I allow
the anger to swell with a compulsory
heartbeat. I remember meticulous seconds
scouring our phone records, realizing
your death began its spiral with Ms. W.
Advice to race away sent you dashing
from the prescribed safety of medication
that leveled your broken will to whispers.

Scuttling the avenues of our city
to see if your old life could erase
the prick of pain from her words.
You took her sentiment to mean
the end, but she never knew you.

I can point fingers at men and their
abusive, coveting cream pie cravings,
but she was as much a perpetrator
as any of the wicked worms who'd
enter the insanity of your room.
At the end of the day, I blame her.

As I hang the necklace to adorn
the wall next to the desk, I can
smell the hovering allure of coffee
grounding the kitchen with rich perfume.
I can follow this stained memorial in the air
to pour a cup for you…but you're gone.
And I miss you dearly as I blame her.

Beccaphoenix, the Crockett, & Ms. Bradley

This entry is only for you. There was a moment after Jean had passed that I'd thought I'd found a second soulmate in my life — you. One resonating soul is rare, but to experience that connecting tissue twice appears to be an extremely rare occurrence for any lifetime. It felt as if we'd known one another for an entire epoch of seasons as I came to admire your appreciation for Kandinsky and Pollock — artists who seemed to mirror your mixture of chaos and establishment. The array of wildflowers that shined within your brown eyes captured me, and the music you adored seemed fit to me like puzzle pieces who'd touched their cherished partners. Ultimately, you left four times, with the final exodus being the coldest.

Each time you left you stripped a small fragment of heart from me and absconded it to the side without care or regard. You once parted ways to explore a relationship with an old boyfriend, only to return with promises so empty an endless void seems to bear more markings of concrete corners. You folded me away with callousness through a lens of supposition and assumption based upon your own experiences that bore no resemblance to who I am or was. I realize now that you never expressed exertion to uncover who I am as a whole. Rather than communicate your mind, you destroyed mine.

In the end, you left me broken without a care. You left wreckage and it never bothered you. You forced me to hide from you that beautiful resin of myself that was born of her. Had you allowed my heart to blossom in full, we might've found our forever sharing coffee and pizza within the most remote arenas of the world. We could've been explorers in life, discovering the globe and one another for all time beneath angelic halos and swollen sunsets. You promised your heart but took mine instead.

As I write this I think of endings and the last kiss. I was never rich enough and never saw the exact moment where I couldn't feel you anymore. Torn is a proper word. Dust is an apt description for how I crumbled. Spiraling is what you left me with as the blackness consumed me with the subtle touch of your vehement fingers. Evil is a harsh tone but resides within the tenor of your voice and the wallows of your deep brown eyes.

Tricked, used, and duped are all words that stir the recipe you fed me for months. You once accused me of lying to you when you found the blog I kept. You accused me of still being in love with her, taking what I'd written to heart without noting the date of the last entry or considering that a blog is where I vent and express. It's not necessarily how I feel explicitly, but a way to unravel my own head without troubling others. You accused me of lying about my feelings through words, completely overlooking the simple fact that my voice on page is uniquely different than how I express myself vocally. The truth is that it was always you who were lying. It was you who used me for nearly a year.

I loved you. You never loved me and there's no remorse within you for that crime. It's the only truth I know. The only truth aside from the absence of Jean and all she ever was — a beauty you'll never earn nor hope to become.

Ms. Armstrong

I've always been a "hopeless romantic". It's cliché to utter such a sentiment about myself, but it's the truth. If I were to apply psychoanalysis to this soulful condition I've carried for much of my life I might attribute it to living with my dad and his alcoholism. Within those subterranean caverns of my heart I — perhaps — wanted to be something other than him. To love someone with a true partnership and lifelong devotion. He cheated on my mother during his alcoholism and, rather than revealing this to my mom, he told me instead. It developed into a situation I had to cope with, and I spoke with this woman at length. It was uncomfortable. She was a waitress at Denny's.

I've always carried this "faith" encircling my notion and belief in the passion of love. For me, it's a partnership between two people built upon an inimitable intimacy and lifelong devotion. It's enjoying the good times and bad, crafting a foundation of memories that fulfill the finest hours of the concluding years of vivacity and adventurous existence. Weathering hardships, along with sharing those cherished seconds, solidifies and glues two souls together with a potency that is impermeable to any outside force. Best friends and confidants. Trust and wholeness in their fullest potentials. Love is ever-changing and one reshapes and modifies to suit the other creating a lucid perfection. I would've changed for you. Love is pure pain sugar.

Each time you left my life and quit I believe I lost a little bit of that faith and trust in love. A piece of the trust I held for you and your words diminished diminutively over time. I'm not sure if you can place yourself "in my shoes" for a moment, but imagine being on the receiving end of learning that the person you've fallen in love with — the one you believe to be a second, rare soulmate in life — leaves you to explore a relationship with an old spark from years before. The words pierced me in ways you never understood, and I feel I hid that well.

I truly appreciated our weekend after Christmas. It was a gift I thoroughly enjoyed and the fact that the locale held significance with your past was never lost upon me one bit. However, the next week it didn't "feel" like a gift any longer. It felt as if I were expected to meet some bar of which I was wholly unaware. Perhaps I'm wrong about that but, maybe, knowing that might illicit some understanding within your core regarding my reactions. They were less than stellar and unfair. Were I a stronger person I'd have simply walked away, but I'm a slave to being in love. I loved you with everything about and within myself. A part of me still does.

I never lied to you, but I felt you did. In retrospect, I suppose you didn't. I simply didn't understand that you were seeking something casual, while I was with you for a lifelong commitment. You had "one foot out the door" the entire duration, while I was firmly grounded within "us". Had I known your true intent, I might have exercised caution with my spirit from the very beginning.

I tend to personalize everything. I take in and hold myself accountable for every disaster or mishap in my life. I've always felt this way, and it probably stems from my father as well. It's why I still can't forgive myself for Jean's death. Her suicide is my fault — I fundamentally feel this way and never released the impression. It's why I was such an outstanding, active alcoholic for many years. It's why I keep attending meetings today. Perhaps you never knew that about me or cared to notice.

There are two songs that come to mind this morning. One is a video you sent, and it remains within a special slice of my character even though the sentiment delivered was one I misinterpreted — Judah and the Lion. The other is just surrounded by the canvas of the chorus and I'm not sure if you like them anyway.

I'm sorry for my part afterward, and I'm sorry I fell in love with you. I'm sorry those feelings still linger within my heart. I placed a weight in your life you were not ready for — nor wanted.

In the end, you stated that you felt I had to be coaxed into sex. There was never any truth to that statement and, I believe, fundamentally, you knew that. There was never any truth to the way you viewed me; no truth in the way you surmised; zero truth within the walls of your assumptions. Live with that the knowledge of your falsehoods — and the damage done.

The Smiles
on the Wall

There's the peak over your shoulder,
your gaze somehow roping me in with
the expertise of one who's wielded the
lasso for centuries. Ashes and ghosts
escape the lips and curvature of your cheeks,
and I find myself caged. Your soul resides
just behind me, as your fingers caress
my shoulders and ward away the crying
of the day. There's the one with your eyes
glowing beneath pink skies across faded
brows and the peak of your nose invites nuzzling,
contained voices. You whisper to me within
late, dark hours where remorse haunts me
through the endless, stripped universe.
Nothing makes sense without you anymore
and you're so out of reach yet contoured around
my frame as I succumb to slumber.
I remain in love. All my life…in love.

I Regret My Own Shit

I woke up too early once again.
In these hours of the night my
mind wanders backward, as if
falling into the caress of a cocoon
whose sole purpose is to haunt me
with you. Your laughter reverberates
through tiny cracks of this small
apartment, lifting me away from
all things real into some obsessive,
fabricated memory where you've
awakened to find me, bend gently
over my shoulder, and don a loving
kiss. Just as you did mere years ago.
Through every hangover of darkness
…I miss you.

www.ingramcontent.com/pod-product-compliance
Lightning Source LLC
Chambersburg PA
CBHW021703110726
47902CB00007B/2039